MW00883526

NECESSARY LIES

Richard Edgar

Copyright © 2018 Richard Edgar

All rights reserved.

Cover design by Shaw Fan Khan.

This is a work of fiction. Names, characters, businesses, places, events and incidents are either the products of the author's imagination, or used in a fictitious manner. Any resemblances to actual persons, living or dead, or to actual events, are purely coincidental.

For Lia, with love.
And for all the Lias in the world.

NECESSARY LIES

Chapter One - Always Tell the Truth
1

Chapter Two - I Hardly Knew
13

Chapter Three - More Homework
18

Chapter Four - A Funeral
23

Chapter Five - Dinner in the After
32

Chapter Six - Misfit Toys
36

Chapter Seven - On the Street
50

Chapter Eight - Lia, Edited
56

Chapter Nine - First Blood
60

Chapter Ten - Vicky
64

Chapter Eleven - A Normal Week
67

Chapter Twelve - Two Assaults
69

Chapter Thirteen - Rehab
74

Chapter Fourteen - Learning Again
77

Chapter Fifteen - Spycraft
82

Chapter Sixteen - George
86

Chapter Seventeen - Ravynscroft
91

Chapter Eighteen - Real Life in Paradise
99

Chapter Nineteen - Somebody needs to tell this
101

Chapter Twenty - Chris' Tale
105

Chapter Twenty-One - The Conspiracy
110

Chapter Twenty-Two - Beginnings
113

Chapter Twenty-Three - To Old Times
117

Chapter Twenty-Four - How... Amazing
124

Chapter Twenty-Five - George
128

Chapter Twenty-Six - Trading
131

Chapter Twenty-Seven - Command and Control
137

Chapter Twenty-Eight - One More Thing
142

Chapter Twenty-Nine - The Why of Things
145

Chapter Thirty - Exile
152

Chapter Thirty-One - Living Alone
155

Chapter Thirty-Two - Cilla
158

Chapter Thirty-Three - Unrequited Oxytocin
163

Chapter Thirty-Four - Moving in Together
172

Chapter Thirty-Five - Job
176

Chapter Thirty-Six - Going Home, I

180

Chapter Thirty-Seven - Going Home, II
182

Chapter Thirty-Eight - So, How to Say This
186

Chapter Thirty-Nine - Lia Counterplots
194

Chapter Forty - For a Black Op...
202

Chapter Forty-One - Shakes
207

Chapter Forty-Two - Craving Affection
212

Chapter Forty-Three - Thumbing
219

Chapter Forty-Four - School
226

Chapter Forty-Five - Managing
230

Chapter One

Always Tell the Truth

Miranda, 2014

"Always tell the truth," Mom told me.

So I did. There are lots of exceptions to the rule, it turns out. If they don't ask, it's okay not to tell them. There was something about *Don't Ask, Don't Tell*, I don't know, but it's a phrase that gets kicked around at the endless potlucks that are the building blocks of lesbian culture. Which we attended as kids, because what else were they to do with us?

And I don't really have any idea where I'm going with this, so I'll just write some stuff and edit later. Or not edit later. Authentic and raw is a kind of truth, isn't it?

Every family has these little dialogs they settle into, I think. After Mom says "Always tell the truth," The next sentence out of my other Mother's mouth, usually, was, "It's way less complicated than keeping track of stories." By which I think she meant lies. And I am with her there. Remembering who got which version of things is usually more work than it is worth. Making it up as you go along is easy. Remembering who you told what about this is not.

But there's something about being a teenager that just breeds complexity. We have to look at everything from at least six points of view (aren't there always more points of view you haven't thought about?), tell the other other side of the story, worry about how each cardboard bit part character feels about the whole thing. Maybe it's because I was raised by lesbians, with endless chatter among the adults about who felt what about which horribly awful thing somebody else did to her. Or said to her. The more the intense the feelings, the more the horribleness. Horribility. I'm sure there's a word for that.

~

"You ready?" said Vicky, leaning against a locker two down from mine.

"Feet off the wall," said Mr. Dean, who happened to be walking by. He didn't stop to see if she did it or not.

"I just think it's cute, in a skirt, to put one foot on the wall when I lean," said Vicky, when he was gone.

"Yup, ready," I said. I hefted my backpack, and like many days before, we walked out of the school entrance next to the cafeteria, out to the street, and turned right. Almost everybody else goes left, toward the Pike, towards the street corner they named the town of Tysons Corner for. Where there are buses and stuff. A few kids actually live in the apartments down our way, but we walked through there, and into the industrial park thing beyond.

We started comparing notes on people we knew. "Jim?" said Vicky. He lives next door to me. So maybe I know him a little too well or something. "What? I think he's cute," she said.

"Sam?" I suggested. Another guy we'd gone to grade school with. "Kinda dreamy, I think."

"Also some kind of weird fundie or something," said Vicky. "D'you ever think about girls?"

"Duh," I said. "Both my moms are lesbians, of course I think about women."

"Somebody in particular," said Vicky.

And I got all shy because... Well, because.

Right again, down the middle of the industrial park. There's a pub in the back corner. "Sometimes I tell people we go to the pub for a drink after school every day."

"I do, too," said Vicky.

"The moms took me there once. It's not much to talk about." The path through the woods connects to the parking lot behind the pub. It's not much of a forest, and half of what isn't street is a garden. When I started high school there, the moms walked me down the street, rang the bell at the last house, introduced me, and got permission for me to walk through there.

Otherwise it's like an hour in a car driving around everything through the traffic and stuff. And it's not the same way as to Susie's school, so it'd be a longer commute for one or the other of the moms, dropping me at Marshall.

"Anyway, we're home," I said, changing the subject. I hoped.

Vicky stopped at our house on the way home most every day. It'd be an hour or so before her dad got home, and this gave us a chance to hang out or do homework or whatever. It was turning into spring at last, and the browns were just starting to turn to pastels. I put my gloves in my coat pockets, just in case I still needed them tomorrow. It's still chilly walking to school every morning.

"Oh, so there's this book Mr Dean suggested might help with the genetics stuff," said Vicky. "I couldn't find it so I stood there til the librarian got it for me."

"And you probably got a lecture on the Dewey Decimal System for your trouble," I said.

"And how to use the computer catalog. Like, why is this not in my phone?"

"Any good?"

"The phone?" asked Vicky.

"The book, silly."

"Oh, that," she said.

"Oh, that," I said, and she looked up to see me grinning at her.

"You drive me up the walls as much as my sisters do," she said.

"I like your sisters," I said.

"Yeah, well, you don't see them that often. You should come over sometime." Vicky lived about half a mile away, on the other side of the bridge over the Beltway, in a house stuffed completely full of girls. Plus two parents. Her dad was seriously outnumbered.

"The book?" I asked.

"Oh right. It's got lots of cool pictures in it," said Vicky.

"And you didn't read the words," I said.

"Hey. I was getting to that."

"Tomorrow," I said.

"And tomorrow, and tomorrow," said Vicky. "Quoting poetry isn't going to get the biology homework done. Which is too bad; I kinda like Mr. Dean. He's pretty cool for a teacher."

"Sighing over the teacher also isn't going to get the homework done," I said. "So I was kinda wondering..."

"Uh-oh," said Vicky.

"I mean, most of the adults I know, except your parents, in my personal life, I mean, they're gay. Or something."

"Jim's parents are straight," Vicky pointed out. He's the kid next door we used to play with.

"I... Well, I have my doubts about Ms. Grossman," I said. I'd seen her looking at Mom in much the same way that Mama does. Or that Tom guy she works with, what's his name? Professor DeSantis. Dunno about Mr. Larkin, Jim's dad. "Anyway. The teachers? Not a single one of them."

"Your adult friends are mostly friends of your parents," Vicky pointed out, "who are friends because they're gay."

"Point," I said.

"Pretty much all the gay people from around the area, I think," said Vicky. "The women, at least." She had been at the house sometimes after school on Potluck Night, when I think every lesbian couple in the county was at our house. "And if the teachers did happen to be gay, coming out can get them fired."

"That sucks," I said.

"What does it suck?" Vicky said, quoting Mr. Dean, and then bumped her head on the table during a somewhat overwrought performance of laughing her ass off. As the textpeople like putting it (They abbreviate, of course; it saves your thumbs). It totally served her right. "Ow," she added.

"So, homework," I suggested.

"Huh. I wonder if being gay is inherited," said Vicky. As if she'd just thought of it.

It's hard, remembering that our lives are so different, despite spending so much time together. She was walking around the dining room, rubbing the bump on her head. "I've always liked this picture," she said. The long-delayed wedding picture, in a neat little frame. With me in the picture, holding flowers. Because I was, like, fourteen already by the time my parents were married.

"My folks have some wedding pictures around," Vicky said. "They look so young..."

And we looked at each other from across the great divide. I mean, like, duh, if a woman is going to have, what, ten kids? And she's straight? She'd best get started right out of school. Which would make her not much older than we are now. When the picture was taken, I mean. Meanwhile, gay people wait decades and finally it's decided. Over there across the river. Cherry blossoms on the DC side of the Potomac. Not here. Never here.

"It's just... people usually get married before they have kids," said Vicky.

"Straight people do," I said. "Sometimes."

We looked at each other a little longer, each wondering what kind of alien she'd become friends with.

"Gotta go home," she said. "See ya tomorrow morning."

"Good night," I said, a little more huffy than I needed to be, given the circumstances.

And she went home. Dinner was served. Mom was her usual

chatty self at the kitchen end of the table. Susie was... being a kid, and after a few words from Mom she settled down and actually ate her spaghetti.

Mama was... Wow, this is going to get confusing. Let me just use their names, shall I?

Mom is Lia, who's an academic, teaching biology and doing lab work at George Mason, here in Virginia. MacDonald. They have different last names. Mama is Sarah Hartley, who's an actual medical doctor and does research on, let me see, fertility. Right, that's it. She works at George Washington University Hospital.

Yes, there are a lot of Georges there. Sometimes the parentals call each other George. Oh, and George Marshall High School.

~

Where were we? Oh right, the night I learned the Family Secret.

Mama--Sarah--was kind of sullen, sitting at the foot of the table, or is it the head? The end farthest from the kitchen.

"What's up?" asked Lia.

"Nothing," I said, before looking up to see her staring down the table at Sarah. I was about to apologize when the Finger of Maternal Wrath shut me right up. It's kind of like a Jedi mind trick or something. Lia holds her finger up, pulls it down in the air, and silence ensues.

"Sarah?" said Lia.

"Proposal," said Sarah. "Gotta get the f... the Institutional Review Board..." I was laughing (silently, because of the Finger of Wrath) about the almost-slipped F-word, so I missed what she actually called the board. "... to approve it," Sarah finished.

"Ah," said Lia. "This again."

"I should have gone into... research not involving human subjects. Something else," said Sarah. "I really really hate this part of my job. They're being helpful, by poking holes that aren't there in an effort that's already behind schedule. We'll be very lucky to get it over to NIH by the deadline."

"What if it's late?" I asked, forgetting the Finger of Wrath.

Sarah laughed, but not from amusement. "*Treated as routine correspondence,* is what the instructions say. I think that means they just throw it out without reading it."

I chuckled, encouragingly. I do like her stories about what she does. It makes more sense to me than pushing microbes around in test tubes, or whatever it is that Lia does. Maybe later in bio class, I'll learn enough to follow.

"Are you working on it tonight?" Lia asked.

"It's out of my hands for the moment," said Sarah. "I should stop moping and enjoy the day." She looked at me. "How's your homework?"

"Genetics," I said. "I'm not getting something."

"May I help?" Sarah asked.

And so instead of washing up, we got out my books and notes and suddenly everything made sense. Frau Doktor Doktor Hartley parted the waves of confusion with her hands and pulled me through. I kind of wished Vicky had been there to see as I saw. Maybe I could explain a little of it.

"So..." I said, when the last problem had been worked. "What's up with sex?"

"Um...," said Sarah.

"I mean, genetically. You can explain the rest some other time."

"Whew," said Sarah. "I was worried. Really, you can ask us anything you need to know."

"I know that," I said. Whether I actually *would* is another question, one she had not brought up.

She explained X and Y chromosomes and stuff. It made sense, fitting into the dominant and recessive stuff in my homework.

"Except..." Sarah said, once she was convinced I understood. "Except for you. You're special, in so many ways."

Moms say things like that a lot, so I had no idea what she was talking about.

"I study human fertility. You know that."

"That would be why the sign outside your department says Human Fertility Institute," I said. Okay, Miranda, it's time to shut up with the wise cracks and actually listen. This sounds interesting. "Sorry," I said.

She smiled. "Well, in some ways you're living proof that the experiments were correct."

"Experiments..." I prompted.

"I can explain at length, with enough words to confuse anybody, including the people who helped make this happen. There's some magic we figured out how do with stem cells and CRISPR." There's this wizard's pose she has when she's pleased with herself. Half smile, arms folded. "But just to say it simply, for once: You are the biological child of two women, Lia and me."

"I... *what?* How? I mean... I dunno what I mean."

I mean, Susie had this kids' book about a family with two moms, and I read through it in about twenty seconds, nodded, and that's kinda the way we are. Heather has two mommies, plus a biodad out there someplace who... the moms never talk about. So of course we wonder who he is. And now they're telling me. I should listen.

"We figured out how to combine half of my genetic information with Lia's in one of her eggs, and how to convince Nature that you should grow and develop. And here you are, alive and kicking."

"So my mama is actually my dad. How... bizarre. I don't even know what to think. I've always kind of wondered who my actual biological father was."

"Wonder no more." She was actually grinning.

"Is that... like, legal and everything? I mean, it sounds risky."

"The IRB didn't need to know, we decided. Sure, it's arguably unethical, but we were quite sure it would work... that you'd be fine, if only you were allowed to be."

"That explains all the extra checkups at GW Hospital," I said. "I figured it was all normal, but Vicky goes to the doctor maybe once a year. And there's less curiosity about her girl parts."

"Smart girl," said Sarah. "Yeah, we needed to be sure nothing we did accidentally gave you any genetic diseases or had other side effects. And I'm happy to report that, at least so far, nothing is out of order."

"Um, yay? I think?" I said. "Oh, and hey, all that teenage boy-trapped-in-a-girl's-body stuff is crap. I had to be a girl, no question, because both of my parents are women."

She looked me right in the eye and said "Right." We are a family of secrets, we tell the truth except when we don't, and I thought there was something a little off about that answer, but it wasn't enough to question at the time.

A question for another day. I certainly had enough to chew on for that day. "I... uh... I dunno what to say."

"We've been meaning to tell you when you were old enough. I don't think I need to tell you that the less said about this outside the family the better."

"Right, I can see that," I said.

"And Susie's not really old enough to handle it," said Sarah.

"I can see that, too."

"You can talk to Lia and me all you want. I'm sure you'll have questions."

"I... it's a lot to think about," I said. Remembering my manners, I said, "Thanks? I think? For explaining all this to me."

"Anything for my Miranda," she said. "You might want to write your thoughts down, like in a diary or something. Off to bed with you now."

"What was that about?" Lia was asking when she met Sarah at my bedroom door.

That's one parental conversation I would love to be the

proverbial app in the phone to overhear.

I sat on my bed for a long time, just cussing. I don't normally, but... I mean, what? Like, I can't even. How? I don't wanna know the details, probably, and I wouldn't understand them anyway, not with just high school biology. What am I... How do I think about... Can't talk about it, even with Vicky. Maybe especially with Vicky. She has a mouth and nine sisters and it'd be everywhere in the county before I finished the sentence. Jeeeezus. Fuuuuck.

Chapter Two

I Hardly Knew

Miranda, 2014

Gah. What to think. Sarah suggested I write a diary, so I did, and it's handy for remembering, but. All the weepy stuff, what am I, a teenager? I mean, really. Put it in the journal; maybe all the tears will stick the pages together so I don't have to read it again.

How do I think about this? The only people I'm allowed to talk to are the ones who did this to me. Who did this thing that created me. It's... like that Charlie Brown comic where Lucy wishes her brother had never been born, and Linus is silent for a frame, and says, "Never been born... The theological implications alone are staggering."

I don't know nuthin about theology. I'm just starting to know a little about biology. The whole playing God thing, making new life that's... Well, it's what parents do, I guess. Just... a little cold and a little odd and... I dunno. I don't even know what I don't know.

Normally Vicky... But I can't talk to her about this. She knows all and sees all that is Miranda, always has, and I figured always would. Well, I figured wrong.

I guess I should let myself into the maternal bedroom sometime before they go to sleep and sit with them and ask all the questions. I don't know what questions. I... don't know. I'll probly cry and I hate that. Sarah kinda looks at me like I'm an alien or something. Your eyes are leaking. Yeah, exactly, Mork from Ork. Lia offers an arm and some tissues and lets me go on about whatever in half sentences interrupted by blubbering.

~

Anyway. There's life to live, breakfast to eat, school to go to. Classes to take.

Health class. The time when they herd us into a classroom with the unfortunate biology teacher, and force us to talk about embarrassing things. Everybody groans, because it's a thing you do. So Mr Dean, a cool guy with more hair than any other male teacher, is standing up there telling us it's okay to ask him anything, even though it's obvious from his body language that he'd rather be talking about lizards or genetics or anything else.

He's cute, I guess, especially when he's talking about snakes. Or feeding the gecko in the glass cage in the science room. It's a little distracting having a six foot long python scoping out the light bulb in its cage while I'm trying to listen to a lecture, or in this case, a discussion.

Of, and get this: diversity. Tolerance. Live and let live. Some people are, like, gay or whatever. Say it with me, everybody, *Like, duh.* It's the 21st century, last time I checked. All together now, roll your eyes. I'm not the only person around with two moms or two dads. Or just one parent because it turned out the other one was gay. Vicky seems fine with it, even though she's Catholic and has more sisters than I can keep track of. Lia says... Well, anyway. That day.

Sam. He was a kid Vic and I had gone to school with for years. We used to kinda hang out on the playground or whatever, until we discovered that we're girls and he's a boy and *eeuw* and we never quite got past that. I mean, some of the boys were... cute. Plenty of time to think about that. Sam... dunno. Not so cute. Well, maybe.

So Sam was kinda pushing back against the Party Line of the Day, which is Mr Dean saying it's okay for people to love whoever they love, and it's important for other people to let them do that, because they have lives and stuff just like everybody else. People can't help who they love. Stuff like that.

"Well," said Sam, and I knew from the smug way he glanced at me it was trouble. "I don't believe in the gay lifestyle." I forgot about the python in its cage.

I dunno if he was trying to or not, but it made me mad. And as Vicky says, a mad Miranda is a dangerous Miranda.

"My moms are gay," I said, without bothering to raise my hand. Mr Dean just kinda let the discussion happen. "Be careful what you say, you're talking about people in the room," I quoted. It's a tactic Lia uses sometimes. And, for her, at least, sometimes it diffuses the situation. I dunno, puts some real skin in the game or something.

"Yeah, well," Sam conceded. "You're not responsible for your parents' poor lifestyle choices."

He could not have chosen more irritating words. I could go on for an hour talking about how it's not a lifestyle, it's your life; it's not a choice, loving whom you love. Can you tell the lady at the potlucks who taught me this was an English teacher? And I don't know what love is, really, except for my moms and when she's not too obnoxious for Susie, my sister, and maybe Vic who's my Best Friend Forever. Some of the boys are cute, comma, but. Not, like, can't take my eyes off them cute.

It seems like all that flitted through my head while I was getting madder. My mouth opened. I glanced at Vicky and stared back at Sam. "Yeah, well," I said. "I'm gay too."

It... I... Dunno why I said that. I mean, I dunno what I mean. It... just kinda popped out. Just like that. Right out loud. In our school culture it's not like the end of the world or anything, but it's... the Real Thing, somehow, Coming Out. And I... Well.

Silence in the classroom. The words echoed in my head and I wanted to die of embarrassment. Sam shut right up. So did everybody else, including Mr Dean, who I didn't dare look at. The bell rang. Thank God.

Everybody packed up their backpacks and walked out. News spreads like the plague and I was so not looking forward to gym class next, down two floors and all the way around the school of course, but I was absolutely sure everybody would have heard by the time I got there.

"Hey," said Vicky, coming up beside me. She pushed me into one of those closed-off doorways, dunno, it's a janitor's closet or something. And she kissed me. Right there in school. "That's the bravest thing I've ever seen," she said.

"Oh, I dunno about that," I answered. "I don't think I'd kiss a girl in the hall. Just for example."

"Honey, you just did," she shrieked, laughing, and ran off the opposite direction.

~

"Hey..." I said, scratching at the open door of the maternal lair.

They were in bed, both lamps on, reading their separate science papers or grading or whatever.

"Miranda," said Lia.

"Can I come in?"

"Long time no cuddle," said Sarah, pulling back the covers so I could climb over her to the spot between the moms. She covered us up when I got there. Lia found another pillow someplace for me to lean on.

"What's on your mind?" Lia asked.

"I, um..."

Silence. Whatever was left of their projects was put up on the bedside tables. Reading glasses folded neatly on top, two pairs.

"You, um..." Sarah prompted.

And the whole story came spilling out in one go. I kinda sorta came out in class today and Sam is an idiot and Vicky kissed me and I didn't know she was gay and come to think of it I didn't even know *I* was gay til I said it and I'm still not sure it's true and there I said it and now I'm going to cry. With relief. That's my story and I'm sticking to it.

Lia put her arm around my shoulders.

"Who here knew Miranda was gay?" Sarah asked.

Lia put her other hand up. After a second or two, Sarah also put her hand up.

Which left me. "Why am I always the last person to know things?" I asked.

They mumbled about experience and when I was your age and being twice as old as dirt (they didn't say that) and, um, pretty soon I was giggling.

"I think it's bedtime," I said.

"Sleep well," they said together.

I shut the door on the way out.

Chapter Three

More Homework

Miranda, 2014

Another night about that time, there was more homework, and somehow things are so simple when Sarah explains them but so impossible when Mr. Dean does it, so we were talking about genetics again. This time Lia had finished with the dishes and Susie was off watching TV or something.

"So, there's more," said Sarah.

"About genetics?"

"Sort of." She was blushing, ever so slightly.

"I don't think I've ever seen you embarrassed before," I said.

She looked up, fidgeted some more, and looked at her hands again.

"I... have a genetic condition," she said. "It's kind of complicated, but it fits right in with your homework, so maybe now's the time to talk about it."

"I'm listening... Should I be alarmed? What's this about?"

"When I was a kid," Sarah started, and then she stopped again. "Well, things didn't develop as they normally do. And so after a while that went on arguably way too long, there were doctors, and then there were more doctors, and..."

"Just cut to the chase, Sarah," said Lia.

"Anyway. There's a recessive trait. So normally there would be two copies of the gene. And let me back up again."

I smiled encouragingly. She's normally so smooth in lecture-mode.

"So normally women have two X chromosomes, men an X and a Y. So it's like men are hybrids. Chickens actually do it the other way; hens have two different sex chromosomes and roosters have matching ones. Aaaand that's neither here nor there."

"It was in the bio book," I said. "It's pretty cool." When your mom is lecturing, you pay attention and make encouraging comments. If she's talking, about something she finds interesting for its own sake, then I'm not being grilled about something I did. It doesn't much matter if you forget three quarters of what she said. Not so, that night.

"Right. So oddly enough there's only a little bit of information on the Y. People by default are female, unless that SRY gene turns on. And then hormones called androgens are made, and stuff happens and they come out male."

"OK," I said.

"The code for the androgen receptors, the proteins that read that signal, is, interestingly enough, on the X chromosome," said Sarah.

"Huh," I said.

"Yeah. Huh," said Sarah. "Now imagine there's a mutation, something amiss with that."

"Riiight," I said, trying to think. "So it's probably recessive; most mutations are."

"Good..."

"And so you have two copies and the other one wins and nothing's wrong." I smiled.

"But it's the X chromosome, so that only works if you actually do have two of them."

"For women. Aha," I said. "I'm still not getting something. You can still pass on the recessive gene to your kids."

"Yes," said Sarah. "So roughly half the kids are XX, and they're female and, as you say, all's well. What about the XY ones?"

"The boys would, um, wait."

"So the XY fetus is developing, and the SRY gene on the Y turns on, makes androgens, and there's nobody home to listen because the receptors are busted," said Sarah.

"And people by default are female, and so they grow up to be women," I said, gathering steam as the sentence formed.

"Exactly!" said Sarah. "Where did we get such a smart kid, from such unpromising source material?" she asked Lia. They say stuff like that around me all the time. With three doctors degrees between the two of them, it's kind of silly.

"Well, not exactly women," said Lia.

"Yeah, I was coming to that," said Sarah. "When I was a kid they examined everything they could find about me, ran expensive genetic tests, found out I was XY but obviously female, scratched their heads, ran through it all again and collectively went *Hmm*. But meanwhile I was humiliated as only a teenager can be..."

"I do hate the doctor's office," I said, hoping I had a little sympathy. Her life as a kid sounded much harder than mine. "The instruments are cold."

"Yeah," said Sarah. She looked away. "They told me I could never have children of my own." When she turned her face toward me again she had that *get out of my way* expression. "But I decided I would prove them wrong. I would prove everybody wrong."

"Work hard, look at the other side--all the other sides--do your homework, and cheat a little when you have to," said Lia, quoting my grandmother. She sounds like a great lady, but I never got to meet her.

Sarah turned to look around me at her wife. "Exactly. I wish my mother had told me that then," she said. "A nice, concise mantra like that would have made all the studying easier."

"Not really," said Lia. "Hard work is still hard."

"Anyway, the condition is called Complete Androgen Insensitivity Syndrome. Just in case you want to read up on it," said Sarah.

"Thanks," I said.

"CAIS. It's easier to remember."

"If you like acronyms," I said. I hate acronyms, and they know it.

"Oh, and..." said Sarah, "you really shouldn't talk about this, any of this, outside the family."

"Totally," I said. "Totally totally."

"Mom?" called Susie from the other room. Her TV show was over.

So Lia went to help her get ready for bed.

"Mama?" I said, when she was gone.

"Yeah?" said Sarah.

"Thanks for... the info, I was gonna say," I said. "But thanks for proving everybody wrong, and working so hard so I could be here."

She stood up, beside my chair, put an arm around my head, and kissed the part in my hair.

And when I stopped feeling like a student who'd just understood a lecture, she was gone, but I had to wonder if I appreciated being buried in an avalanche of information about, well, myself, ultimately, but mostly about my mom-who-is-my-dad. Life kinda made sense, just last week. I remember that.

It's a thing, now. Sitting on the edge of my bed in the dark going Jeeeeezus. Fuuuuuck. Holy information overload, Batman. How do I... even start... trying to feel this?

And there's... something... just out of reach, about the genetics. That I wanted to ask. But it got away.

Chapter Four

A Funeral

Lia, 2013

Dinner out, together. When we still did dinner out together, and it was special. New neighbors watching the kids. And it was time to go home to all that already.

"Your bag is buzzing," said Sarah.

"I'm driving; can you see what it is?" I said.

Sarah pulled out my phone. "Dear Lia," she read aloud. "Is this the Lia MacDonald of CCHS class of 88 (Go! Away! Eagles!)" Then she added, "From somebody named Cris Martin." And she spelled the name.

"Yup," I said. "Clarke County High School. Wow. Send her this: I presume this is the former Kris Martin, of (see above)." I also spelled the name.

Sarah's thumbs obeyed. "Yes," she read from the phone. And then, "Something's come up. Can we talk?"

"Sure," I said, relayed through Sarah's thumbs again. Then we waited. The jingle for new callers was unfamiliar, so I was smiling when Sarah poked the speakerphone button.

"Hey," I said. "That's how the dialog went in high school, right?"

"Hey," came a voice. Edgy, somewhat low, but not by way of tobacco. Soft like unbleached cotton, somehow, and I wasn't sure why that particular metaphor came to mind or just what it meant.

"What's up?" I said.

"You remember Liz White," said Cris. It wasn't a question.

"Of course. I haven't thought about her in years." And then something about the tone of voice alarmed me, even though I hadn't heard the voice in years. "What's happened?"

"She was killed. They think maybe it was an accident." There was sniffling at the other end of the phone.

"Oh my God," I said. "What happened?"

"Details are sketchy," said Cris. "There'll be a service next Tuesday. I thought you'd want to know."

The tension in the voice hid a lot of emotion; that much was clear. "I'll be there. Send me the details."

"I will. Talk to you then." And Cris was gone.

Sarah offered to drive, since I was upset.

I looked at Sarah. "I should go."

The phone buzzed in Sarah's hand. She checked and it was an e-mail from Cris. When we traded seats, she gave me the phone.

I was shaking. "It's hard to live with stress, with the constant threat of... something," I said. "Best not to imagine what, happening at any time, just because. Because somebody doesn't like your face. Because they don't like your lifestyle." I snorted. I don't think Sarah's seen me, crying til I'm all snotty. "It's not a lifestyle," I explained aloud. "It's an expression of who I am." I looked out the window at the shade of the tree beside the parkway. "I keep imagining a lynch mob and what use they could put a tree like that to."

"*Well you could be less expressive,*" I said aloud. I guessed Sarah would recognize the tone as an impression of my mother.

"No, actually, I can't. I tried. And before you say I could have fallen in love with a boy, I tried that, too."

Sarah sat quietly, watching my conversation with someone who wasn't there. She knew not to interrupt these things. I have these meltdowns sometimes, and talk to my mother, who...

"You died, Mama," I said. "Years ago. And now Liz. To be fair, I knew Liz pretty well in high school but hadn't missed her, hadn't thought of her again, until just now, when I heard that she had died."

I paused to find my handkerchief. "Dead."

"What a remarkably final thing. In that most past of past tenses." I sniffled a little.

"Sorry to hear about your friend," said Sarah.

"Me, too," I said.

"You okay?" asked Sarah.

"More or less. I mean, I hadn't thought about her in years, but she was one of the 'misfit toys' with me and two others, back when."

Sarah grunted assent.

"And I realize that whenever queer people die, it picks at my own angst, even if it really was an accident."

"You can't live like that, expecting attacks around every street corner," said Sarah. "If they get you, they get you. Meanwhile, live like there's no tomorrow."

"Or something," I said.

"Yeah, okay, not my most inspired wording ever," Sarah admitted. "Do you have anything to wear?"

"I do have a black dress," I said.

"What you have is a *little* black dress," said Sarah. "I don't know what women wear to funerals these days, but that's not it."

"Point. You want to go shopping with me?"

"Noooooo!" wailed Sarah, who hated women's clothing stores. I laughed, which was, no doubt, what Sarah intended. "But I will if you want. Sometimes it helps to have somebody else look at you."

"It always helps to have you look at me," I said.

"You're just a romantic," snorted Sarah.

"I'm pretty practical. You have to be, to manage academia, kids, a marriage," I said. "Or, says the angst in my stomach, whatever you would call this relationship. Depending on who's asking, and where, and what exactly they want to know."

~

It was midday, the church was silent. I was struck the way the light slanted in from the colored windows. There was a small podium set up with an open book and pen on it, near the entrance at the back. Sarah went on to find a seat halfway down the aisle, but the person with the pen was finishing, so I paused to write in the condolence book.

I watched the previous person walk up the aisle. It was a tall woman in black, who bowed deeply and sat beside a smaller friend, perhaps five rows ahead of Sarah and on the opposite side. What would have been the groom's side if this was a wedding, I mused. The signature said Mo Grant. Above that, Cris Martin, which drew my eye. It had been years.

I walked quietly to the row where Sarah was sitting, instinctively genuflected, and sat beside my partner. I took the hand that was offered. The family was at the front, and more were drifting in.

What I remember about the service itself is isolated images. Sunlight shining through stained glass onto the casket. Lots of black clothing. Words intended to comfort that missed the mark. Music, at once familiar and strange, as if a Christmas carol were set to the wrong tune.

Sarah drove me over to the family house after.

I hugged Mo, who was several inches taller, then turned to make introductions. "This is my... partner... Sarah Hartley," I said.

"Mo Grant," said Mo, shaking Sarah's hand. The gesture looked remarkably masculine.

"Sorry for the loss of your friend," said Sarah.

"Thanks," said Mo. "And thanks for coming, and bringing Lia."

"Of course," said Sarah, probably wondering what else she could say.

"I'm Cris," said the small person at her elbow.

Sarah turned and found Cris staring into her eyes. Sarah returned the gaze, showing my old friends what kind of a person I was with now. Or out of respect. Or something; I didn't quite know. Someone's eyes filled with tears, and I wasn't entirely sure whose.

"Sarah," said Sarah. "I'm Lia's wife."

After some finger food and some hugs for the family, Mo said, "Let's blow this joint. Delmonico's?"

"I have the Harley," said Cris. "It's not exactly..."

"Ladylike," said Mo. "It'll do. You coming, Lia?"

"We'll follow in the car," I said. "No way I'm riding a motorcycle in a dress."

Mo shrugged, handed her bag to me for safe keeping, grasped her hem in two hands, kicked her leg over the motorcycle, snuggled up tight behind Cris. She tucked her bag between her belly and Cris' back. They roared down the street in a cloud of black taffeta.

Sarah followed at a more civil pace.

"It's like Pizza Night with the Misfit Toys," I said, pulling Sarah onto the bench outside the hostess station at the bar.

"Except..." said Cris, a tear escaping, running down unadorned face, and dripping from chin.

"Yeah," I said. "All of us in black, and the Age of the Goth came and went in the meanwhile."

Mo chuckled.

"Harley, party of four!" shouted the hostess.

"Wait," said Sarah. She recited the names: "Cris Martin, Mo Grant. Did I miss somebody's name?"

"No, no," I said. "It's a game we played. Liz was always particularly creative with the names."

"Name your poison," said Sarah. "I'm buying."

"You seem like a woman of some taste," said Cris. "Surprise me."

So Sarah ended up dropping most of a hundred on fine Scotch.

"To Liz, who finished the race first," said Cris.

"Liz," said Mo.

"Liz," I said. Three friends stared, each at a different spot on the table.

"She haunts you all still," said Sarah.

"Yeah," we all said at once.

"Tell me about her. One thing each," said Sarah.

"She taught me how to mislead people, how to lie," I said. "And that there are things so true they're worth lying about."

"She understood a boy who needed to be a girl," said Mo. "Better than I did myself."

"She put me together again, in some very real ways," said Cris. "And held the little group together, even when we were all going different directions."

"Different directions?" Sarah prompted.

"We hardly knew ourselves, then," I said. "Coming out, for me. To myself, which was a surprise, because I needed to come out to her."

"There's a story there," said Sarah, smiling.

"Starting the long journey from male to female, by way of Kuwait and the USMC," said Mo. "What a long strange trip it's been."

"Starting the long journey from victim, little girl of a punching bag, to... something... else... Anything else. Leaving everything behind, just being me," said Cris. "You know, I never could understand why you wanted to be a girl, Mo, when I wanted absolutely anything but."

"We should have traded," said Mo.

"I would have done it in a heartbeat," said Cris.

"And what about Liz? Was she going somewhere?" asked Sarah.

"Dunno, really. I guess I was too caught up in my own issues," I said.

"You hardly had any issues," said Mo. "Little Miss Good Girl, acing all your classes."

"Until I fell in with the wrong crowd," I said, laughing. "Present company definitely included."

"We knew each other since primary school," said Cris. "Back when I was a girl."

I looked at Cris. "Long time ago."

"And miles to go before I sleep," said Cris.

"Food? Or are we good with just liquor?" asked Sarah.

"I suppose I should eat," said Cris. "Wouldn't do to fall off the Hog."

"Hm," said Mo. "These folks do breakfast all day and night. That's new."

"So is drinking whiskey here," I pointed out. "If we're staying, I'm needing the bathroom."

Chapter Five

Dinner in the After

Lia, 2013

Cris and I returned from the bathroom. "There are two floors here now," I announced. "And they have an ungendered restroom upstairs."

"Cool," said Sarah.

"You'd think, in the twenty-aughts, that they'd be more common," said Cris.

"I guess it's still a huge political thing," I said. "That, or having single-seat places, which isn't that practical for a busy restaurant. Anyway. I interrupted. What were you girls talking about?"

Mo sat up just slightly straighter and smiled. "You know, ancient history, and modern revisionism. The usual sociable going through the motions stuff."

"Hardly usual," Cris laughed. "At least for me."

"I have the impression there's not much usual about you," said Sarah. "And I'm sorry if I've offended," she added, to fill the resulting silence.

"It's true," said Cris. "Since I got the girl shit kicked out of me, and never really wanted anything male, it's been kind of uncomfortable, camping somewhere in the middle. Like a nomad, between oases. Or something."

"Tell us about you two," said Mo. "All gay-married and everything."

"Or, as we like to say, married," I said.

"How did you meet?" asked Cris.

"Drag show. I surprised my lab taking several of them out to a gay bar. I suppose they knew, but I wasn't exactly out," said Sarah.

"I used to go there occasionally just to be me, unedited," I said.

"You're a little too frighteningly good at the self-editing thing," said Cris.

I laughed and stuck my tongue out at Cris. "Anyway. Cute woman, as you can see, who can dance, is slightly drunk, and approachable..."

"Cute is as cute does," said Sarah, smiling at me. "And I couldn't overthink and talk myself out of it with her tongue in my mouth."

"Zapwhampow, in a word," I said. "And the rest is history."

"Herstory," said Mo. "Counting you both, that is."

"Itstory," said Cris. "I just had to say that out loud, once."

"I kinda like it," said Mo.

"I do, too," said Cris. "Not that I like the 'it' thing in isolation."

"No," said Mo.

"So how does the state border work? Are you married on both sides? What does that even mean?" asked Cris.

"It's complicated," Sarah and I said together, and then all four of us laughed.

"We have an ever-growing briefcase full of papers on the subject," I said. "One copy in the trunk of each car, just in case."

"Yikes," said Mo. "Somebody should smack down the hammer of justice on those people."

"Not sure it would help," said Sarah. "We'd probably end up listed as terrorists or something."

"I'm in, whatever's going down," said Mo, quietly.

"Me, too," said Cris.

"We should keep in touch," I said. "We don't live that far away."

"I live in the District myself," said Mo. "Sometimes I go visit vets who don't have anybody else. *Semper Fi* and all that."

"That's cool, Mo," I said.

"And, uh, just kinda bringing some order to the streets," said Mo.

"Super-Mo," said Cris.

"You're no slouch yourself," said Mo.

Cris smiled, and I realized it was for the first time all afternoon. It seemed very obvious that, whatever Cris was doing now, *victim* was no longer part of the script.

~

"Tell me about the Misfit Toys," Sarah said, in the car on the way home that night.

"We were a high school clique, in a lot of ways," I said.

When the silence got long enough, Sarah tried again. "I want to know about high school age Lia coming out," she said. She looked at me while she was waiting for a traffic light.

I looked up from where my hands seemed to be wrestling in my lap. "Okay," I said, and sighed.

"Maybe it's too soon, after..." Sarah suggested.

"Well, no," I said. "It'll do me good to remember happier times."

Chapter Six

Misfit Toys

Lia, 1987

We went to school together at Clarke County. There was this funky bunch of meeting rooms upstairs in the back of the school library. I'm not sure what else they were used for, but our very small advanced French class met there. There was a second exit, normally locked, no doubt to satisfy the paranoia of librarians over lost books. If you wanted to steal library materials, you had to do it under the watchful eye of the front desk person. I think this is before they had those electronic gate thingies at the exit, but it was also before people wore backpacks everyplace. Simpler times.

So that provided a really interesting little spot at the top of the backstairs, just outside the locked exit door. There was a small, half-lit hallway that went in under the French room from near the cafeteria. It was so far out of the way that I don't think anybody but the janitor knew it was there.

It was a perfect place to be out of the public eye, for misfits like us.

"Hey," I said, turning the corner and climbing the second half flight up to the landing outside the door. I think I was kinda sweet on him.

"Hey," said Maurice.

"Howzit?" was the next item in that foreign-language-class dialog that we always recited on meeting.

He flubbed the next line. The funky light coming through the little window in the door showed a new bruise on the side of his face. "Dammit, Maurice, they beat you up again."

"Yeah," he said. He was shaking.

"You're safe here," I told him, but saying it out loud left me pondering the tactical situation in the silence of my own head. The Offensive Linemen wouldn't really fit here more than one at a time, and we had the high ground. I blame war gaming with Maurice. I imagined a flying kick in the nose, wondering whether the shape of the lug soles of the boots I wasn't wearing that day would imprint on James' face or not.

"Oh, you're here already," said Kris, coming around the corner on the landing halfway up the backstairs. "You're so quiet. I'll just make some noise," she said, putting down her stuff.

Maurice chuckled softly. Kris sat down sideways a couple steps from the top. The dress code hadn't changed, but since Kris came back to school, I never saw her wear a skirt again.

Footfalls announced Liz, who despite obedience to the dress code flopped down facing Kris. "I", she announced, "have an announcement."

More silence, this time anticipatory.

"I am a thespian," said Liz. "I've hidden it all my life, and now, at the advanced, well, okay not that advanced, age of seventeen and a half, mustn't forget the half, I'm coming out of the... backstairs. I got a part in the play."

"Congratulations," said Maurice.

"I thought you said lesbian," was what escaped my own lips. My hands writhing in my lap suddenly required my full attention. But when I looked up, they were not looking at me.

"It's a pun," Kris explained.

"You're smiling," I said. "No, don't stop because I noticed." There was an odd expression on her face, so I stood her up and gave her a hug.

"Nobody ever hugs me," said Maurice.

So Liz hugged Maurice, and we had a group hug and then somehow I was hugging him, face to face, and I was sure he could tell somehow that I thought he was cute and had fantasies about exactly this, well, he and I... or maybe Kris... uh... and, ahem, I'm not finishing that. This is me, shutting up now. Cut to the slapstick. The landing at the top of the stairs is small, and we were not paying attention to where our feet were.

The fire alarm went off, somebody stepped off the edge, and we fell down the stairs together.

"Let's go up," I think Kris was saying. The lights were suddenly bright and I could read her lips but wow is the alarm loud in a little space like the backstairs. "The door unlocked." They helped me up and put my dress together again. So not only did Maurice feel my body against his, he also got to see kind of a lot of it.

So we went into the French room and waited out the fire drill. I'm sure we all deserved to burn in... school, if not in actual hell, for not evacuating like good girls (and boy). But nothing came of it.

"This is nice, just us here," said Maurice, when the alarm quit. "Isn't it, Kristine?"

"Just Kris," said Kris. "I'm cutting off my..." and she shrugged elaborately, leading my deviant mind to suggest *hair* and then

Please God No... before she filled in "second syllable."

"Mo," said Maurice. "I like it."

"Lee," I said. "I've always envied the guys their monosyllable macho names. Joe. Tom. Hank."

"Huh," said Liz.

Everyone laughed.

"And besides that, I think I'm giving up anything else that's gendered," Kris muttered to herself, just loud enough to overhear. "Like pronouns and gym class." Himself. Theirself. Oh. It'd probably be themself.

"Good luck in French," I said.

~

The name changes did wonders for Kris and Mo. They dressed more or less the same in t-shirts and button-downs, slacks and shined shoes. They even got the same haircut. The four of us hung out in nice weather in the courtyard, on one little dead-end stretch outside the math classrooms on the third floor balcony. One of the cool kids started calling that "the Island of Misfit Toys," and we liked that enough to adopt it.

The assistant principal was not amused by androgyny. Mo was intimidated until he saw the sullen defiant look in Kris' eyes. There's something about that "been there, done that, have the scars" persona that'll scare off even the gruff ex-Marine school disciplinarian. Nothing he could mete out would compare with the hospital. Or the anteroom of Hell from which it was the exit.

In bad weather or sometimes just because, we'd end up in the backstairs. And sometimes the memo didn't circulate. One nice day, Mo and I happened to be in backstairs, while Liz and Kris were admiring the birds from the Island of Misfit Toys. Mo was upset by yet another run-in with administration, one where Kris wasn't around to out-cynical the powers that be.

"I dunno how she does it," said Mo.

"Knowing for a fact that she's seen worse, I think."

"I guess. I admire that," said Mo. "At the same time it creeps me out, trying to imagine how she got that way."

"The world is full of horrible things," I said, "and you can find them if you look. Sometimes they find you."

"You're scaring me," said Mo.

"I'm scaring myself, too. Can I snuggle up closer?" So I did that. It was reassuring, the body contact, feeling Mo's body heat.

And, um. How to explain what... Teenagers. Body heat. How very confusing it was to see Mo's eyes looking at me, from under Kris' hair. A fine and private place. And even though I had a crush on Kris, since long before she went away, since ABBA. Since Springsteen. Oh, God, we played *Hungry Heart* to death. Long before the Indigo Girls put queer in pop culture, to guide our way.

Mo was close enough. While waiting for Miss Right, Mister Right Now would do, apparently.

There was some kissing. It was nice. I mean, who knew? There was some more kissing. And, um, stuff, like, y'know.

What with the small landing and more important things to pay attention to than our feet, we took another tumble down the stairs together. No harm done. The clothes, upon careful inspection, were rumpled but undamaged. Mo ended up with a bruised rib, possibly caused by the bannister. Somehow I turned an ankle, a little. A quick trip to the bathroom to touch up my face and fix my hair, and I was good for the rest of the day.

Emotionally, though... We really weren't prepared for that. I know I wasn't. The taste of his kiss... became an obsession. And Mo was... I dunno. Setback in whatever pilgrimage he was taking. Or something. I couldn't afford to care, being way off-balance myself.

It was awkward, hanging out with Kris and Liz in the Island the next day. This misfit toy was on one end of the foursome, and Mo was on the other. Carefully not looking at anybody. Especially not each other.

"*What??*" Liz demanded, picking up on it instantly. I could have been wearing a big red *A* on my blouse and there wouldn't have been any more of a delay. Kris looked up from her introspection, her fascination with her hands, and whether her thumb would block out the entire fountain from this high or not.

"We..." I said.

"Kinda..." Mo said.

"No," said Liz. "You didn't. You really did?"

Tiny nods from both ends of the gang. An odd smile appeared on Mo's face; it turned up a little at one end and down at the other. Like that Russian guy, at the UN? Gromyko? Wiser, perhaps, but infinitely sadder.

And Mo and I both, and I promise this is the last sentence with that compound plural subject, made a point of never being alone together again.

Somehow just knowing I shouldn't, didn't keep the flashbacks out of my dreams. And it was sufficiently... odd, shall we say... that in my saner moments I had no desire to repeat it. Scratch that. Desire is always insane, and it was always there. No *wish* to repeat it.

So there you have it. I've come out of the backstairs.

"What is it?" Kris said one day at the railing. It was about a month, after... And now *That* has become the dividing point in my life. How did that happen?

"Comes the time of the month when the hormones *reeeeeally* want to go out, get laid, get pregnant," I said.

This brought a visible shudder from Kris. "I know what you mean."

"I'd sort of thought maybe I was being obsessive, not letting it go. But that's really not it. The cerebral end of me is kind of along for the ride here."

"It's one of the monsters in my deep," said Kris. "Staring into the abyss."

"As in looking into the darkness?"

"As in making it blink first."

We stood together, staring down into the fountain two flights below.

"I'd ask you to hug me, but that's how I got into this obsession in the first place."

Grim laughter and a nod.

"We should do something fun. How long since the last pizza

night?"

Kris was not to be drawn on questions of the passage of time. But my own reckoning came up with a *Before That* time. Maybe six weeks. Ago, not six weeks BT.

"Have anybody's dietary preferences changed since then?" I wondered aloud.

"Don't need to think about it til we get there and order," Kris pointed out.

"Hey, everybody," I announced cheerily when Liz and Mo joined us. "Pizza night!"

Kris looked at Liz. Kris looked at Mo. Kris nodded, sadly, and stood next to me at the rail, between them.

~

There's that seating area at Delmonico's where you wait for the hostess to call. We arrived one by one, squeezed onto the bench, all the monosyllables. Kris was there first, then Mo, Liz, Lee. Though I have to say that Kris and Mo actually took to their monosyllabic names, while I was, just, shrug, Lia, like always. Lee sometimes, but mostly not.

"Bananafish, party of four!" screamed the hostess.

Mo and Liz looked at each other. "That has to be us," said Mo.

I was too appalled to agree. The game is that the first person gives a name and everybody else has to recognize it when it's called. I knew Kris had read Salinger, and that Liz and Mo probably hadn't. All that talk of staring into the abyss, plus the title of the story where Seymour Glass killed himself... It was too much.

So our fun night out was surreal. Liz was trying to sit as close to Mo as possible, resulting in an otherwise funny in a slapstick kind of a way migration counterclockwise around the table. I was trying to watch Kris to see if she was more morose than usual, staring down some new monster. And participating in the migration, trying to stay a little farther away from Mo. At the same table with him and the girls was fine, but next to him, not so much. Besides, my shirt buttoned that way and he probably had a view.

"Toppings?" I demanded, when the waiter came our way.

"Plain," said Mo. "Topless."

I gave him that dirty in-your-dreams-mister look, remembering it was anything but.

"Peppers," said Liz. "Hot ones."

"Onions," said Kris. "Anchovies. Rubbing salt in the wounds."

"You only get one," I said.

"Right," I told the waiter. "One large pizza. Onions, hot peppers, extra cheese, and for my choice, the sausagefest."

Liz broke out laughing. "I could *not* believe they put that on the menu." Blushing bright red, she was unable to stop laughing.

"Pitcher of Mr. Pibb," I added over the noise. It was a soft drink once. Do they still make it? Gosh it was awful stuff. The waiter shrugged and left us.

"You coming to Karate tomorrow?" Kris asked Mo. They'd been doing martial arts together.

"Yeah, I guess," said Mo.

Kris looked at me, and I started to babble. Anything to fill the vacuum. Free associations and all that.

"So I am reading and Mr. Pibb is sitting in my lap and he touches noses with me and head-butts my chin and snuggles in." I neglected to explain that he was a cat. "And so he starts that kneading thing, and I wish he wouldn't do that to my boob, especially when, um y'know, we're all girls here, right, so anyway he snags a claw and unsnagging him practically takes my shirt off and my Dad is grinning and Oh My God, I'm so sorry, Mo, I wasn't thinking."

"It's okay," said Mo. "I like being one of the girls."

"I don't," said Kris.

There was one of those moments when everybody else in the noisy restaurant fell silent at once, and even the clock stopped ticking. Kris and Mo looked at each other, baffled.

"Particularly big weather we're having this month, isn't it?" I said, just to change the subject to absolutely nothing. "I think I'd run to the bathroom and never come out except just now I'm up against the wall like the first people come the revolution and... And I'll just shut up now and die of embarrassment. Okay?"

Kris began to laugh. Not shrieking out loud with disbelief as Liz had done, but with some sympathy, and with admiration about how tangled up in free associations I had managed to get myself without any help from them.

"How did you know? About, y'know, Mo. And me." I asked Liz.

"You were not exactly subtle," she said. "You really need to learn how to lie, if you wanna keep secrets. Especially from us."

I pondered this for a while. "Need to know? That kind of thing?"

"The fact you have a secret is itself a secret." This time it was Kris, and I turned to her in surprise.

"You have secrets?" I asked.

There was that thing she did sometimes where her lip quivers and liquid essence of pain drips from her face.

"Right," I said, conceding the point. "I'm sorry." And I took her hand, tentatively, wondering when the last time I touched her was.

"Lia," said Liz. "Look at me. Eye contact is important. If you're not looking at me, it's like a dog, broadcasting that he got into the garbage again."

I laughed.

"You don't have a dog, do you?"

"No," I said. "You know that."

"Okay, look me right in the eyes and tell me something outrageous."

So I took Liz by the hands, raised my eyes to hers, stared her about halfway down, and said the first outrageous thing that came to mind. "I'm gay. I love you."

Liz stared back at me, not flinching. "That's not even a lie," she said. "At least the gay part isn't."

"I just figured it out," I said. "Right now. Talking to you."

"I have known that for years," said Kris.

"Why am I always the last one to find out these things?" I demanded.

"Not the last," said Mo, miserably.

"There's too much going on at the table right now," I said. "Mo, I'm sorry; I didn't know myself. Kris, wow. Just wow. I'd hug you but I'm stuck behind the table. Liz, what are you talking about?"

"Give me your hands again," she said. "Look at me."

So I did.

"I'm flunking out of high school," she said.

"Can you flunk out of high school?" I asked. "Oh wait. That was a lie, wasn't it. I'm so confused."

"Yes," she said. "To all three questions. You can flunk out. It was a lie: I'm not. And you certainly are confused."

"Where did you learn all this?" I asked.

"From my dad, mostly," said Liz. "He's been telling me whoppers since I was in Kindergarten. Maybe longer. Teaching me to be skeptical, he says."

"Your turn," said Liz. "Pick somebody, tell them a lie."

"Mo," I said. We looked at each other across the table. "It was... my first kiss," I said. And then I blushed.

"Bzzzt," said Liz. "Also true. We're trying to teach you how to lie sincerely. You're not even trying."

This only made my face even redder. And I couldn't look at Mo again. When I did, I said, "It was wonderful."

I glanced at Liz out of the corner of my eye. She was smiling.

But there was a tear sliding down Mo's cheek when I looked at him.

"I hate this game," I said.

"You don't have to talk about your sex life," Kris pointed out.

This came as a revelation to me. What else would somebody want to keep secret from her friends?

"Girl. Look at me. If you're really gay, you need to learn to not just blurt it out to anybody within earshot." Liz glanced at the people at the next table. "And to not let on that you have anything worth hiding. It's not their business."

"Suddenly life's no fun," I said. "Speaking of which, Bananafish?" I said, turning to Kris.

"*A Perfect Day for Bananafish*," she said. "Salinger."

"I recognized it, yes. You okay?"

And I got that *stare down the abyss* stare, right in the eyes. I looked back for as long as I dared. It's dark in there, behind those eyes. And she blinked.

"Yeah, I guess," said Kris. "I'll organize the next pizza night.

How about that?"

"Cool," I said. "Shall we set a date?" I had no idea how to cope, but making plans for the future, specific plans, seemed like a step forward.

"Wooooooo!" crowed Kris, laughing. "I have a date with Lia," she sang two or three times, in that tune that has annoyed generations of adolescents. Using the two-syllable version of my name, to make it scan. I swear Kris is always three or four layers deep in indirections and innuendo.

"You do!" I said. I glanced at Kris as she paused, contemplating another round of pizza.

Chapter
Seven

On the Street

Lia, 1987

We spilled out onto the street, bellies full of pizza and soda.
Around the corner and we almost walked straight into the offensive
line. Kris belched loudly. Soft drinks will do that. It could have been
timed better.

"Are you belching at me, runt?" asked James. He easily weighed
twice what Kris did. Two of them outweighed all four of us. And
there were five of them, who did everything together. "I'm talking to
you, boy," he said, when she didn't respond.

I dunno if he noticed, but she stood in front of him, hands at her
sides, knees slightly bent, utterly relaxed. In my third eye I saw the
snake coiling for a strike, but apparently he did not.

"Wait," said Mo.

"Oh, look, they're twins. Identical, I think. Are you a girl or a
boy, runt?" James said to Mo.

But having two targets was more than he could concentrate on,
and none of his buddies seemed to be interested. Covering his jaw
with his left, he swung with his right at Mo. Kris was interested in
surviving, not fighting fair, so she kicked him in the crotch, hard,
and then met the collapsing giant with a karate fist in his solar
plexus. He landed more or less on top of her, but we managed to
separate them before he was capable of doing anything further. We
ran off while his buddies tended to him.

And we spent a quality hour with the Vice Principal the next day.

"You're a smart girl," he said to me. "AP Physics, that's impressive. I could never do science." He laughed nervously. "Getting tangled up in fights would be a black mark on your permanent record, Lia."

I envied Kris her ability not to care about these things. Men in ties and offices have always intimidated me.

"And you, Liz," he continued. "You're doing well, promising future, all that. Who's going to marry a girl with bruises on her face?"

Liz squirmed as he intended.

"Maurice. Get a haircut, my man."

When Mo started to reply, he was cut off.

"There's a recruiter from the Marine Corps on campus tomorrow. I've set you up with an appointment. It would do you good. Make a man out of you."

Kris stirred, looking up.

"And Kristina," he said, adding not one but two syllables to her name. The last one isn't even correct. "We meet again."

She stared at him, letting the psychic pain flow from her pores, from her eyes, sharing her misery with the world, focusing it on Mr. Kauffman.

"Well," he said, looking down at the papers on his desk. "I

approve of self-defense courses, especially for girls," he said. "You really mustn't use those skills unless your life is threatened."

Kris breathed, but made no other response. She leaned forward, ever so slowly, grasping the front edge of her chair with both hands, between her thighs. I watched the muscles tense. Her nostrils flared. She inhaled. She exhaled. Then I watched her relax. "We're done here," she said quietly. We stood up and walked out, even though we hadn't been dismissed. I felt like a puppet on strings, and it was abundantly clear who was pulling those strings. If I hadn't been to the bathroom just before we went in, I would have wet myself.

"You," I said to Kris, "are a badass."

But she was stuck someplace in the hell inside her head. I thought about giving her a hug, letting her know we were there for her. But I wasn't absolutely sure she wouldn't respond with violence. That dark place she went? It scared me.

Even though class was in session, we walked single file around the courtyard, through the cafeteria, and into the backstairs. I considered a detour to the bathroom to vomit for a while, just because, but decided not to. We had already established that my bladder was empty.

"I'm shaking," I said, when we were settled.

"I'm not sure which was worse," said Liz, "facing James in his wrath, or sitting quietly in Mr. Kaufman's office."

Kris looked up, focusing her eyes on something other than the Vice Principal for the first time. "Kaufman is not a threat," she said. "We understand each other." She paused. "Well, I understand him. I have no idea what he understands, except he doesn't fuck with me."

"I think that's the first time I've heard you use the F-word," I remarked, trying to bring some levity in to the situation.

Kris turned her head to look at me. The pupils in her eyes shrank as I watched. A tiny smile appeared on her lips. "I'm full of surprises," she said. "You okay, Mo?"

"I...," said Mo. "I dunno. I think so."

"Should I believe you?" I asked.

"No," said Mo.

~

Liz was driving; we picked up Kris and Mo after their karate class. As promised, Kris organized pizza night, which was no problem since we were all together anyway. And we dropped off first Kris and then Mo at their houses. Liz had a book she wanted to give me, so we hit her house next.

"What are your plans?" said her dad, looking up from a book. It was already 10 o'clock.

"Sleepover," said Liz. This was the first I'd heard of it.

"Lia doesn't have a backpack or anything," he pointed out. I had slept next to Liz's bed dozens of times, but always brought my own jammies and toothbrush.

"We'll just sleep naked. Have hot sex. It'll be fun," said Liz.

"Okay," said her dad.

I was, shall we say, flabbergasted. His expression was unreadable; part smile, part bemusement, one eyebrow raised. Liz hustled me out of the living room and down the stairs to her basement lair before I could unlimber my mouth, start babbling, and embarrass us both.

"Don't mind me," she said. "He doesn't believe a word I just said." She found the book. "Although," she said, turning to look me in the eyes, "there's nothing like telling the exact truth to be disbelieved. Beats lying any time."

Something rolled over in the pit of my stomach, but in a surprisingly pleasant kind of a way. My fingers tingled where they touched hers, handing over the book. I leaned closer, my nose beside hers, and we kissed. Putting my arms around her neck I managed to knock the book into the back of her head. It's difficult to protest when your lips are sealed to someone else's.

And then I pulled away. Before my body could do any more talking to hers. Or listening, more to the point. "I, uh," I stammered. And then the babbler engaged. "I would *love* to, Liz, but, um, school night and I... God you're beautiful up close and warm and curvy and I like your fingers in my hair and your bed's right there and you even got your dad to... agree... kinda sorta?" Okay, that line of reasoning, babbling, broke the mood.

"I'll get my coat," I said after a silence. She let me slip out of her arms, took me home.

~

So there you have it, Sarah, my love. The creatively non-fictionalized version of How Lia Came Out To Her Friends (And Herself In The Process). It's quite the tale, don't you think?

The Misfit Toys drifted apart. I got into the University. Liz's dad, contrary to her expectations, was actually listening, and didn't want me around the house any more. Mo joined the Marines, with a lot of badgering from his dad and Mr. Kauffman. He told me just before he shipped out that he liked the scarlet and blue dress uniforms. "It's a way to be flashy without being gay," he said. "A wimp. I like what admitting you're gay has done for you."

Which was, I devoutly hoped then, precisely nothing. Learning to live with the secret made me more aware of how I looked to everybody else.

Kris dropped out. I think. The occasional letters or cards, each from a different city, spelled her name differently.

Chapter Eight

Lia, Edited

Lia, 2013

"That's not how Mo told the story," said Sarah. "I was asking her about things while you and Cris were powdering your respective noses. In the bar after Liz's funeral."

"Mmm?" I said.

"It all sort of sounds like high school excuses and bullshit," Sarah said. "It reminds me of some of the inept tales Miranda has told us." She drove on in silence for a long while. "Mo is apparently still kind of traumatized that she... Wait. I dunno how to tell this story. And it feels ridiculous to ask, but telling stories about trans people from before, do you use their old pronouns, or their new ones?"

"Or just try to avoid them altogether, like Cris," I said. "Make up new ones. Alternate. Some damn thing. I can't keep track and I stopped trying. Trans people are complicated, and kind of touchy about that kind of thing. Pronouns and stuff. I mean, I like Cris and all. And I'm glad Cris can articulate a way of being that appeals to her. Him. Pick both or neither. I had a crush on her back when that just wouldn't quit. One of those where I never dared tell her about it, because, um, we were scared teenagers. Or something. And by the time I came out she wasn't really a girl anymore. Ships passing in the night."

Sarah was smiling when she glanced at me from the road. "Anyway, Mo says that he didn't manage to rescue Cris from, who was it..."

"The football team," I said.

"That's it, yeah," said Sarah. "And I can feel myself editing the story as I piece it together, so neither Mo's version nor yours will agree with it."

"Memory is a tricky thing. I think the very act of recalling something edits it."

"You remember that discussion we had about secrets?" said Sarah.

"How can I forget?" It was far--too far--into our relationship when she told me about her genetic condition. I think that was when we learned to cry out our anger for each other, together.

"And you said you thought you didn't really have secrets, from me, I mean. From the world outside, sure."

"Go on," I said.

"I think you keep secrets from yourself," said Sarah.

"Huh," I said. "Like whatever happened to Cris."

"You didn't want to know, so you never found out. Or if you did, you walled the whole story up in the cellar of your mind. Edited to make it bearable, or something," said Sarah. "I know Mo was haunted by that night for years, and it's a large part of why she's doing street work now: atoning for that, somehow."

"Huh," I said again. "I'm pretty sure Cris and Mo were doing karate classes together when we were in high school."

"So you said, yeah. Mo certainly picked up a lot of martial arts stuff in the Marines. But it seems to me it makes sense if there's only one actual fight with the bullies, and that Cris kind of never came back to school, or not for long, afterwards."

"I'm pretty sure I remember seeing her kick him in the nuts," I said.

"Mo remembers you all running away," said Sarah. "And it seems implausible that the rest of the bullies would just stand by like cardboard cutouts doing nothing if she did. Kick him. She being Cris in this case. Gah, this is confusing."

"And far from being haunted by the experience, I just went off to college and acted like a good girl. Well, except for the gay thing. That much was real."

Sarah stopped at a traffic light. She looked at me for a long moment. "I hope so, my love."

"It's a little late for you to have doubts about that," I said. "What with a marriage, a mortgage, and two kids. Who have two moms."

"It came out a little more skeptical than I intended," said Sarah. "But I do worry, I guess. Being written out of your world because of who I am would suck. I like having you in my life, Lia."

"You like having me in your bed," I said, grinning. "And to bear your children and then manage them while they grow up."

"All true," said Sarah. "And it might come in handy having badass people like Mo in our corner, if those briefcases of legal papers don't do the job."

I nodded solemnly, the light changed, and the moment passed.

"I didn't get much of a chance to talk to Cris," said Sarah. She-- gah, I'm doing it again--they... Starting that sentence again. It seems

an interesting thing to get to know... and I need another pronoun.
Cris."

I was chuckling in sympathy. "I do remember the pronoun wars
from high school, especially in French class, where the poor
teacher's actual job was teaching us correct grammar, whatever the
queer political niceties. Although, come to think of it, much of the
political correctness in language came along later. Maybe I learned
to be sensitive to it from Cris. And I'm doing again, editing in things
from years later."

"I'm not all that excited about getting the story straight," said
Sarah.

"She said *straight*," I said.

"She did, yes," said Sarah. "I just kind of want you to be aware
that what you remember might not be exactly how it all happened."

"Subconscious memoir editing," I said. "Apparently I'm more
devious than I ever knew."

"Yet another reason why I love you, Lia," said Sarah.

I was skeptical.

Chapter Nine

First Blood

Miranda, 2014

So, yeah. Like I said, news travels fast. All the cool kids, they wouldn't talk to me any more. Vicky, who had outed herself as much as I had, hung out with me, and that was cool. It was kinda like being thirteen again. Being social outcasts...

She said *out*, says one of my moms in my head. It's lame, but it is kinda funny.

Being social outcasts was kind of freeing in a way, once we got used to it. Nobody cared about us, and we didn't care about them. That was the theory at least.

But there was Sam. Somehow he felt I'd wounded his manhood somehow. I really can't understand that I did anything to him; he wasn't really my friend before, and he really wasn't my friend now, and so that's that. Apparently I'd made him look bad in front of his people? Lia tried explaining how fragile masculinity is, and how dangerous it is if you break it. But you know? If I'm gay? Why should I care? It's not like I'm going to be dating men or anything. Boys. Whatever they are.

And the thirteen year old Miranda just went *Eeeuw, Boys* in my head. I'm sure the then-Vicky would have laughed with me.

So we're standing at the rail in the courtyard, Vic and me, after fourth. It doesn't pay to be on time for lunch, so there's a few minutes of just being, together.

"I kinda miss hanging out with you in the mornings," I said.

"Four whole periods of not being in the same class. You'll live," said Vicky.

And I turned to look at her. My glasses kind of blocked the side vision. There were footsteps behind me, and something hit me in the back of the head. My glasses flew off, and of course I tried to catch them, and I was also whirling around to see what was going on and my fist kinda sorta connected with Sam's nose. He hit me back, and I remember seeing his notebook go over the rail, and hearing it hit.

Two seconds. The world went silent, except for the breeze scattering the pages of Sam's notebook in the courtyard below.

"You're bleeding," said Vicky. "And I caught your glasses." So we went to the bathroom to clean up, but I was still bleeding, so Vicky took me to the school nurse. Who of course told the principal's office and my guidance counsellor, Mrs. Dempsey, who's a useless excuse for an adult human.

The nurse got the bleeding stopped and Mrs. Dempsey called both of my moms to tell them, actually got ahold of Sarah, and Vicky insisted on coming home, so there we were, in the kitchen, completely stuffed with people. Vicky and Susie were in one corner, and Mrs. Dempsey brought along some guy from the school system.

"Scoot forward, and put your head back on the chair," said Sarah. She double folded a towel to put under my head. "I want to see the dressing."

She's the doctor, so sure, whatever. Normally she's doing research at work and not fixing up patients, but she'll do in a pinch. She cleaned out my split lip, decided I didn't really need stitches, taped it together and got it to stop bleeding. Again.

Lia finally got home about this time, and got Vicky to tell her the story about what happened. Sarah's good with the actual tending of wounds and blood doesn't wig her out or anything, but for organization in a crisis, Lia's your mom. Well, she's my mom, but she's the one to depend on for that kind of thing. Or something.

She sent Vicky upstairs with Susie when everybody had heard the story. I was trying to hold still for the medico, so I wasn't much help.

"There are a few forms we'll need to fill in," said Mrs. Dempsey's shadow. He introduced himself, I think, but I was a little distracted. Big guy; I remember being a little afraid of him in the way that monsters in the movies have shadows bigger than they are themselves. His forms didn't seem to have spaces on them for the names of two moms. And this is Virginia, after all, and you'd think there would be some progress with the new millennium, but no. So I'm living in a potentially unfit home, because my parents aren't married, or my mom is living with another adult who's not her something something and even though they love each other and work well together and Virginia is for Lovers (it says so, right on the bumper sticker), they're not married only because it's illegal and it'll stay that way for the rest of forever, world without end, Amen. Because... battle flags. Rednecks. The Lost Cause. Slaves. All men are created equal (no mention of women), writes the guy from just down the road a piece, except apparently he meant some are more equal than others. And those guys still write the rules and run things. It's all so *1984* and George Orwell and last century and can't it *please* all be over now.

"I have a bad feeling about this," said Lia after she'd showed Mrs. Dempsey and her friend out. "People like Mr. Fisk make me worry."

"He seems like a harmless bureaucrat," said Sarah.

"But he's the kind who needs something in every box on his form, whether the form fits real life or not. I'm sure our family broke his form, and the database at Central School, in several interesting ways." Lia looked up to see Vicky and Susie reappear.

"Is it safe to come out now?" Vicky asked, smiling at me. I tried to smile, but it hurt.

"Yeah, it's just us," said Lia.

"You going to be okay?" Vicky asked.

"I think so?" I said, glancing at Sarah, who nodded.

"I should probly go home then," said Vicky.

"Thanks for bringing Miranda home," said Lia.

"No prob, Dr. Mac," she said.

"I'm hungry," said Susie, when the door was closed.

"Food," said Lia. "I knew I forgot something. Can you manage soup, do you think?" she asked me.

Chapter Ten

Vicky

Miranda, 2014

Vicky was all concerned and stuff. It was kinda cute, her waiting for me just around the corner from the assistant principal's office.

"You have to tell me everything," she said.

So we went back to the scene of the crime, standing together at the railing on the second floor of the courtyard. "Mr. Douthett," I said, kind of lisping so it sounded like Dousett or something. And I had to laugh. I guess I must have bit my tongue along with the split lip. "He was pretty harmless. I was surprised, actually."

"I guess kids getting gay bashed is enough of a thing that the administration noticed and doesn't want to get sued, or something?" Vicky suggested.

I looked at her. "What planet do you live on, girl?" I asked. "Maybe more to the point, where do you get your news?"

"What?" Vicky said. Not like, I didn't understand you *What*, it was one of those What are you talking about *Whats*.

"This is the Confederacy of Virginia," I told her. "People get elected to the school board by making homophobic slurs. Not to mention city and state offices."

"If we go up one floor and look out the open side of the courtyard, we can see the Washington Monument. This is the twenty-first century," Vicky announced. "Equal justice for all and stuff."

"Unless you're black or gay or live in Virginia," I said. "Is my cynicism showing?" I asked, making a point of checking my skirt. "I hate it when that happens."

"The very fact we were talking about it in health class last week is progress," said Vicky. "Don't you think?"

"Maybe," I admitted. "Not to change the subject, but I'm going to change the subject."

"Okay," said Vicky.

"I don't think I ever suspected you were gay," I said. "Until you hustled me into the corner and kissed me in the hallway."

Vicky turned sideways to face me. "It was just the bravest thing I've ever seen," she said. "Verbal fencing with the Sams of the world, sticking up for yourself. And the killing blow was admitting you were gay, right out loud. How could I not kiss you? I fell in love right there, in two seconds."

"Love at first..." I said, trying to smile and holding my split lip together. "...um, something. We've known each other for years, compared notes on the boys, hardly ever talked about getting crushes on girls at all."

"Can I tell you something?" Vicky asked. "I didn't know either one of us was gay until that moment. I wonder if coming out is always this violent."

I checked to see if my lip was bleeding. It wasn't. It was my new tic, fingering the wound.

"Not violent like that, though I guess I should wonder that, too," said Vicky. "Sudden, is what I meant. I went to class that day like any other day, just being me, never actually thinking about stuff like sexual orientation. And before the next class started, wow, I'm gay. Who knew?"

"Who knew?" I echoed. "Apparently both of my moms did. Which, um, huh. How could they know when I didn't?"

"Weird," said Vicky.

"Weird," I replied. We batted the word back and forth a few times, gradually distorting its pronunciation.

"Wee-ard."

"Wye-ard."

"Speaking of wired," Vicky said, suddenly nervous, "You wanna go out for coffee sometime? On a date, like?" She was blushing.

"I'd like that," were the words that came out of my lips, really quietly. "Thank you."

"Whoosh, hooray, and um, can I kiss you?" said Vicky all in a rush.

"Split lip," I said. "And besides, kissing a girl in school is how we got into this mess in the first place."

"I wanna keep doing it. With the same girl, of course," said Vicky. "But I'll wait til it doesn't hurt."

"Thanks. And I'm sorry I called you a mess. Called us a mess."

"Hush up, or I'll kiss you anyway," said Vicky, grinning.

Chapter Eleven

A Normal Week

Miranda, 2014

I want to try to remember that special week, when all was more or less right with the world. It was spring; flowers and trees were blooming. Sure, we were the only out gay people in the school, and that was so weird that nobody knew what to say to us, so pretty much nobody said anything.

We hung out at school between classes when we could, had lunch together, walked home together. We had nervous butterflies in our stomachs together, anticipating date night. It seems so precious now. We made out in my bedroom, waiting for the moms to come home. We had dinner with each others' families. I learned the names of all of her sisters, which had confused me for years.

And it seemed the sun was a little brighter and the rain a little sweeter.

The day came at last. We walked over to the coffee shop after school instead of coming home. The moms thought it was sweet. I was a little scared... I mean what to talk about? What about the fact that I don't actually like coffee? But at least they had people behind the counter who would doctor it up to hide the bitterness.

Vic found us a table in the window, where we sat together in the afternoon sun, holding hands under the table in one lap or the other. People walked by, mostly not paying any attention. Some people smiled. Some people we knew waved or shook their heads.

I suppose we found something to talk about. I remember the debit card. Vic said it was new, and she had trouble figuring out how much money she had on it. We kind of bonded over the mathophobia. If that's a word. And my lip was enough better that she kissed me there in the sun, tasting the extra stuff in each others' drinks.

"Vanilla," I said.

"Cinnamon." she laughed and wiped her lips.

And we went out for a little walk before we had to go home to dinner. There's a little park outside the shop and the sun was shining on the bench and it was nice. She was nice. Everything was nice.

"I guess we hafta go," she said at last.

"Yeah," I said. "This was nice." That word again, echoing in my head.

We figured out how to walk together, in the same slouch, walking in step, synchronizing the heel skip of our shoes between steps. We held hands. I guess in the South that was provocative. Hell, just being me is provocative in the South. As Vicky said, within sight of the Washington Monument, you'd think... But then you'd remember that Old George owned slaves he willed to his wife, despite all the talk of equality and freedom. Never mind all that. Being with Vicky was nice.

Gravel underfoot. I looked up to see Sam grinning at me from behind the steering wheel. Vic yanked on my hand really hard, and I felt something snap.

Chapter Twelve

Two Assaults

Lia, 2014 and 1987

"Lia?"

"I must have drifted off," I said. "What were we talking about?" I have these... spells? When things from my childhood get mixed into whatever's going on today. Thin places, maybe, where the past and the present aren't all that separate.

"Vicky was telling us about the accident," said Sarah.

And Vicky repeated her description of the scene. "We came out of the coffee shop. Maybe a little bit wired. I should do half-caf, but I forget. Anyway, you go around the corner and there's a little alleyway that cuts through the block and there's some gravel in the gutter. I was thinking the footing might be treacherous. We looked up and there's this roaring engine noise, and I reached out for Randa's elbow but I missed. He didn't. I had my phone in my hand and snapped a few pictures. And called 911." She paused for a sob. "I'm sorry, I should have..."

"You did well," said Sarah.

I was thinking of a time, maybe midnight, I was young. A few friends, spilling out of a pizza joint, around the corner, where... Some kind of nightmare happened.

"This woman came out of the crowd, sat on Miranda, holding her down, telling her not to move," said Vicky.

"That'd be Mo," said Sarah. "She's told us the story."

I remembered Mo going down that night. Cris stood for a little longer.

"She asked if I was hurt and I said no; she told me to call 911 and I said I had," said Vicky.

"You did well," said Sarah again.

"That's what Mo told me," said Vicky. "If only..."

"You can't think like that," Sarah was saying.

If only... If only Liz was still alive. Wait, that didn't happen that night. It's all so confusing.

"It's all so confusing," Vicky said. "I remember blood in the gravel, filling in Miranda's footprint, after they took her away."

"Mo and the ambulance guys left you standing there?" Sarah asked.

"There was a cop, but yeah," said Vicky.

There was a cop. After the football guys ran off. Maybe he ran them off.

"I found Miranda's phone," she said. "Gave it to the cop. It needed to be polished or something, wipe the grime off, but he said no."

I remembered Mo's glasses getting broken and stepped on, just out of her reach. I hurt my knees, I remembered that, too. The gravel, the dirt, being ground into the skin. My hands also. There were bandages and bright lights, later. It was so dark.

And some of those scars on my face. The ones I always tried to cover by wearing my hair close around my face.

"Is Miranda going to be okay?" Vicky asked. She was trying not to cry. Sarah handed her a box of tissues.

"It'll take a while, but yeah, I think so," said Sarah. "I think in a week or two she'd like to have a visit from you."

"OK," said Vicky, taking another tissue.

"Are you okay?" Sarah asked.

Are you okay, I heard, over and over again. Bright lights in my eyes, a splitting headache. Somebody picking gravel out of my hands and knees. I think so, I said... Was that out loud? Or was I screaming inside my own head? Or maybe I was screaming out loud and telling myself I was okay. It's important to be okay.

"Yeah," said Vicky. "Oh, let me send you the pictures from my phone." This gave the two of them a shared goal, overcoming technology to accomplish something.

"Say that again?" Vicky asked Sarah, who repeated her contact information.

Say that again, somebody told me. Maybe I was screaming out loud. I'm okay, really I am.

We can help if you let us, they told me. Let us help you.

"We went shopping that afternoon," Vicky said. "Didn't really buy anything, but it's fun to look."

We went shopping, Liz and I. Just to look. She knew all the best stores around, including this funky hippie store where you could get interesting stuff for cheap.

"We're kind of cheap," Vicky was saying, with a smile.

She took me there, once a season, whether we need it or not, she would say. I thought that was funny the first six times she said it. Oh right, that dress. It was risqué, for the times. Hems had gone up, gone way down, and returned, but that wasn't the problem. It kind of tied on and my hair tickled all the way down, because of the backless thing. Sort of double layered, purple flyaway wraparound; more to it than met the eye. And, I think... I wore it that night. I remember that.

And then I was in a hospital gown, the kind that opens in the back. Hands in bandages so I couldn't do anything about it not quite closing. What happened to my dress. They must have it here someplace.

You don't remember much, do you? The cop.

What? What don't I remember? They like, totally examined the rest of me. We don't talk about that. We don't think about that. They gave me something for the headache. Antibiotics for any infections. Dad came around with some clothes. What happened to my dress. It was so hard getting jeans on over the knee bandages, without functional hands. And we went home, right? Right?

You don't remember much, do you? Dad. He and the cop looked at each other.

"Thanks for coming," said Sarah.

"Sure thing, Doc Hartley," said Vicky. "Is Doc MacD gonna be okay?"

Are you going to be okay? It's important to be okay.

"Yes," I said. *It's important to be okay. Especially when you're not.*

Chapter Thirteen

Rehab

Miranda 2014

Rehab was a blur. I saw Sarah every day; she made herself part of my care team, and the docs let her, even though there was some grumbling about it. Letting a mom work on her own kid apparently violates their rules. But I guess I'm special. A lot of those same docs had been involved in the never-ending rounds of physical exams, trying to figure out if I really was a normal human person, despite the odd circumstances around my conception and birth.

I asked Lia once, after a talk through *Heather Has Two Mommies* and a little too much exposure to the Christian culture that seeps from the red southern soil... I asked her if I was a virgin birth.

She inhaled sharply, glanced at Sarah, and shook her head no.

I shot a questioning look at Sarah, and she also shook her head no, as if to tell me not to go there. So I didn't. Biologically, kids have a mom and a dad. Socially, I had two moms. So there must be a biodad out there someplace. It was much later they told me it was actually my other mom. Sometimes, just between us, I would call Sarah "Dad" after that. She let me do it, though there was a lot of lesbian hen clucking about need to know and secrets and not letting on that there even is a secret. "In this particular case," Lia told me, "the truth is so unbelievable that people will happily never even think to question their assumptions."

Anyway, rehab. There was a lot of mumbling among the docs when they thought I was sleeping or whatever about how much steroids it took to... do whatever it is they do. Make me into he-man or something. Stop swelling and inflammation, I think Sarah told me. "Well, I was kind of expecting that," said Sarah. And it turns out she's the same way.

So, y'know? That transgendered friend of the 'rents, Mo, who apparently picked me up out of the gutter and got me an ambulance that day... She would happily sit with me in the hospital and work with me in rehab, telling war stories. She was a marine, and she spent a lot of her time visiting vets who came home damaged somehow. So the medical thing was normal for her.

Anyway, we talked about her, some, too, and taking hormones. I suppose everybody's curious, about how the other sex lives, and what it would be like to change.

"You've met Cris, I think?" she said.

"I haven't met a lot of the people I've met," I said.

"I'll bring them around sometime. She was a girl when I knew him in high school," said Mo.

I parsed that for a while.

"And, uh, bad shit went down and he gave up on her gender altogether."

"I get it. You're alternating pronouns," I said, pleased to have figured it out.

"I try to do what she says when I'm talking about him. It seems respectful," said Mo. "Me, I just changed over once. And when you're big and fierce and have medals, people listen."

After she went away, I wondered if the hormone thing would even work for me. Something else to quiz Sarah about.

Lia came around, now and then. When they were making me

walk with a walker, I went out to sit on a bench in the garden one day, and she was waiting there with Mo. And Cris. Cris was kind of... round, with a nondescript haircut and a middle-range voice. Comfortable shoes, slacks, a shirt with buttons.

"Should I remember you?" I asked. "My memory has holes in it like that... cheese... with holes in it." I had the word *Swiss* when I started saying that.

"I'm Cris," said Cris. "I was a friend of Mo and Lia when..."

"When you were my age and recovering from..."

"Yeah, I try not to think about that," said Cris. "Your body heals, as much as it can. Your mind also, in different ways, with less visible scars. I'm not sure your spirit ever quite recovers."

I nodded. It seemed sage advice, and even if I didn't understand it then, Cris inspired respect just by being themself, and so I filed it away for future reference. "A fact I memorized," is how Lia would describe that: seems important even if it's not understood, so you remember it for later.

Lia was... kind of shell-shocked, I think, by my accident. And Susie was... missing. And nobody would talk about that, putting me off until I would be stronger, sometime. Obviously something bad, and I think Sarah and Lia kind of blamed each other. You live with lesbians long enough, you can read the tone, even if there are no words.

Chapter Fourteen

Learning Again

Miranda 2014

So I learned how to walk down the hall, without sweating bullets. Eventually, without a walker to lean on, or even to catch me when I wobbled. Most of my words came back, though they're slippery, like those little swimmy weasel things? Skittering away just after I decide I need them sometimes. Otters.

Mo was still coming around a lot. I think Lia was living in an apartment nearby, with Sarah. I dunno what happened to the house in Virginia, or to Susie. But they were fighting a lot, my moms. When she thought I couldn't hear, Sarah would tell Mo that Lia was "nuts" or "delusional."

Mo would make reassuring noises about how hard it was losing your kid.

"She's my kid, too," said Sarah.

"Yes," said Mo. "Yes, she is. And you're doing something about it. She can't. She's frustrated."

What they were doing about it, I couldn't imagine, in part because I didn't know what "it" was. Cris was involved, for sure. They'd talk in murmurs sometimes, forgetting that invalids have ears, even if the brain between them isn't quite working right. She's fucking scary. There's pain in his eyes that I recognize, a grim determination not to be the victim she was when he was a girl.

After talking to Mo enough, the alternating gender pronoun thing comes almost naturally. It's like a game for a while, and then you think you can't really remember which one actually applies, or if either one does. She's a man's man, he's a woman's woman. It doesn't matter. And leaving all that behind, plus those black belts she earned in whatever it is exactly he does. I'm glad I'm not in a dark alley with Cris pissed off at me.

The therapists eventually cut me loose, turned me out of the rehab center, in favor of somebody else who needed them more. Sarah didn't quite know what to do with me, since the apartment came with the understanding that they had somebody in the hospital or rehab and needed to be nearby. There was a lot of bickering.

Ms. Grossman, what's her first name... Becca. She lived next door in Virginia. They moved in when I was, what, seven maybe. Vic and I played with their kid, Jim, running around and around in and out of both houses and yards. Eventually, of course, it turned out he was a boy and we were girls and the whole yuck factor turned up. But it was good to know he had my back.

Anyway, Becca came to visit. She was happy to see me up and around and functioning. There was a family meeting in the little apartment; there wasn't anywhere else to go so they let me stay.

"Lia," said Becca. "I have some friends..." She glanced at me, blushing slightly. "You remember Rachael? Rachael Cohen. She came to visit once."

"Oh sure," said Lia.

"She, uh," said Becca, covering her face with one hand. I sat up and started taking notice. "She used to live with Stephan and me. Back before we were respectable professors and stuff. The department there... well, they don't tenure their own, and somehow we managed to work the two body problem and get jobs together, here. The three body problem is well known to be unsolved." She laughed at her own geek joke. Professors are weird. And I know a whole lot of them, including both my moms.

And I had my own memories of that visit. Jim and I were playing outside one Saturday morning, and, well, whatever it is that seven year olds need from their moms, we burst into the kitchen, breathless, Jim shouting "Mom?"

And there was Becca in Rachael's arms, both wrapped up in her bath robe, which was something huge I'd seen Stephan wearing (by himself) sometimes.

"You're naked," said Jim to his mother. At their house, the deal is, if you walk in on your parents naked, you turn around and leave.

"Nuh-uh," said Becca.

"Actually you are, at least from here," said Rachael. It was another of those little moments that burned itself into my mind, a tiny sample of how adult women love each other. We went outside again.

"Rachael," Becca was saying. "She lives in Boston. I've been to visit now and then, when there's a conference or whatever." She was still a little embarrassed.

"Or whatever," said Lia, grinning.

"You could go stay with them for a while, Lia," Becca said.

"It would be good for you to get away," said Sarah.

Serious stuff... I kinda shrank into my corner, wishing I was actually small enough to be the fly on the wall. My moms stared into each others' eyes, not smiling. My heart beat enough times that I lost count. Counting heartbeats and breaths is something the physio taught me.

Lia nodded. There were tears in her eyes. She never cries. "When?" she said, turning to Becca.

"There's one thing I want you to get from the house," said Sarah.

"And then we can put you on a train. Tomorrow if you want," said Becca.

"Tonight," said Sarah.

Becca waited outside while Lia packed up what little she had in the apartment. We had to vacate it anyway. So I packed up my stuff, of which there was even less. It fit nicely in a backpack.

I hugged Lia goodbye at the curb. She got into Becca's car, slammed the door on her skirt, popped the door open, pulled it in, and slammed the door again.

Sarah spared herself the long goodbye, so I was there with my backpack (why did I bring it along?) on the curb, alone in the District, with the sun going down.

I walked along the street to clear my head, which is a futile goal. New Hampshire Avenue. I put out my thumb and some guy in a car with a lot of luggage in the back stopped. "Where to?" he asked.

"I dunno. Key West, maybe," I said.

"I'm bound for Carolina," he said, "It feels like I should say *With a banjo on my knee* or something."

In a day or two I came to the end of the road.

It was going on tourist season, and there was an ad for somebody with a lifesaving certification to work off a boat, so I went to talk to the captain, a woman who was a little younger than my moms. I kinda didn't have any documentation beyond my drivers' license but that was good enough for her. She managed to find me a cheap apartment above a restaurant, in the less touristy half of town where the locals live. And I got to take touristas out snorkeling or kayaking in the mangroves every day all winter long. A girl could get used to this. There's something very real about me and the water, living together.

Chapter Fifteen

Spycraft

Lia, 2014

Miranda finished up her rehab, which left the question of where to go next. Sarah and I were bickering openly by then, blaming each other for Miranda's accident, for Susie, for going from successful academics who'd only slightly bent the rules to... what amounted to interstate fugitives.

Becca came to visit on the last day in the apartment. The hospital and rehab center in the District had a dorm to house families of... I was going to say inmates, but of course Miranda was a patient. She made a good recovery, under the ever watchful gaze of my partner Sarah, among friendly medicos who knew what a special child she is, and were willing to push a few extra steroids just because, monitoring, always, for the desired effect.

"You remember Rachael Cohen," she said. "She came to visit Stephan and me, uh, how old are you now, Miranda?"

"Eighteen almost," said Miranda.

"Right. Just like Jim." Jim was Becca's son; they lived next door to us for years. "Gosh, ten years ago already. She, uh," and it's cute watching adults I know well getting embarrassed about past relationships. "She used to live with us, before we moved to Virginia. Stephan wasn't getting tenure there, though, so we managed to find two jobs here. Three... Well, in physics it's well known that the three body problem is intractable."

Polite laughter is the way you carry off other people's jargon jokes.

"She's living in Boston," said Becca. "You should go stay with her for a while. I've been up there to visit sometimes, when there's a conference or whatever. Her ex has the house, and she's got lots of extra bedrooms. You won't even be a bother." Ex... she... now you have my attention.

I'm sure Sarah put her up to this, so I turned and looked my partner of nearly twenty years in the eyes. How had my life come to this, the four of us, together forever, coming apart at the seams, one by one blowing away. Dust in the wind. But there's a certain calmness that comes from a decision made, so I nodded.

"When?" I asked.

"Today's the last day we have the apartment," said Sarah.

"Tonight, tomorrow, we'll put you on the train," said Becca.

"There is... one thing," said Sarah. "Something I need you to find in the house." She turned to Becca. "Can you take her there, bring her back, and then drop her at the train station?"

"Sure. I'll phone Rachael and let her know you're coming," said Becca.

"You know the place," Sarah said, looking at me.

In the gathering darkness Becca drove up our old street. The house was right where we had left it. I flitted inside, knowing right where it was. A dress, it had been. It had followed me every time I had moved, but had only been worn once. It wasn't in any shape to use after that, but I couldn't let it go, either. There was one of those black plastic bags from the hardware store, which would do. I rolled it up and brought it along.

It hardly seemed to need all the clandestine drama. Becca drove me back to the District. There's a particular room in the Watergate that we, Sarah and I, used to... meet in, back in the day, before we had kids. While we were in and out of GW Hospital having tests and getting Miranda figured out. Sometimes we felt like spies, with all the need-to-know, all the not-quite-legit stuff going on.

She would look at me, say, "You know the place," and hours later I would let myself in to her hotel room. Always the same one. The clerks at the desk expected us. Not so very spylike, but it was thrilling, hanging out there in a darkened room overlooking the centers of power, doing illicit things together. Like lesbian sex. Like conceiving children without a father. Like proving the medical establishment wrong: Sarah could, actually, have children of her own, thank you very much. And here's a thumb in your eye for good measure.

The bedside lamp was on, and Sarah was sitting in the desk chair next to the window, looking out. Tonight her attention was focused across the river. There's a big dark area, Arlington National Cemetery, on what had been Robert E. Lee's plantation before the War. And then to the right a thriving city for the living. For the straight, for the white. For people who can live with the rules there. Which, as it happened, did not include us.

"Do you have it?" she asked, not looking up.

"Yes," I said. The plastic bag rustled a little when I set the dress on the bed.

"Thank you," said Sarah.

She stood up and faced me.

I looked at the reflection of us in the window, the standoff, two lovers, about to part for... a while.

"We will get her back," is what Sarah said.

"How..." I started.

"It's best if you don't know."

"I suck at keeping secrets."

"All the Lias that are my life," said Sarah, smiling slightly. "I do love you, you know."

"It's for the best," I said, half believing myself. Half believing her. Because she was telling me what I wanted to hear. Somehow, Susie... Somehow, love. Never mind how. It's for the best.

I gave Sarah my house keys and went down the elevator to where Becca was waiting in the lobby. She drove me to the train station and waited with me for the next train to Boston.

It was so, so, sad. Too sad to cry, even. It was fitting that it was dark out, that I would soon be hurtling into the darkness, overrunning my headlights.

Chapter Sixteen

George

Wow. A day off. So, what else, I went to the beach. It was a nice day--it's always a nice day in paradise, until it isn't--so I walked the length of the island, stopped off at a store for something to drink, and was waiting in line to check out.

It's a tourist town, and this is the tourist end of the town, so sure enough, the other two people in line were tourists, buying, of course, sunscreen. The guy probably weighed twice what I do and was already painfully pink. The girl had apparently just arrived, was still as white as bread, and wisely taking precautions. I don't think they were together; just happening into the store at the same time.

They both noticed at the same time that, ahem, my coverup was showing more boob than was strictly necessary. It was a hot day, the beach I was headed to was, shall we say, relaxed about these things, and somehow it didn't occur to me to bring along the top half of my bikini. Work is a one-piece suit, because you really don't want to be worried about its togetherness if you're pulling somebody like Mr. Man Mountain out of the drink. Day off? Bikini.

She paid for her stuff and went outside. I did likewise, and since I've been there many times, had change counted out. It took the guy a long distracted moment to finish his business and come looking for me. For us, it might be. Please let her be somebody who'd like to be involved in an us.

He came out through the door, bathing us in one last gasp of conditioned air, looked left, and when the door closed, looked right. So, what the hell, I put my arms around the girl and kissed her. Because it would boggle the guy's mind. It might even shrink his gonads. It would certainly do something to his het privilege male ego. He had the grace to shrug and wander off toward the nearest beach.

"Um, hi," said the girl.

"Hi," I said. "Thank you."

"My pleasure," she said, grinning. "I'm... call me...Const..."

"George," I said, interrupting, it being the first thing that popped into my head. When two or more thoughts rubbed themselves up against each other, George Eliot and then George Sand came to mind. So it's not crazy that a girl who's actually attractive might be called George. "Everybody comes here for a reason they'd rather not discuss. Leaving stuff behind, mostly," I said.

"It's true," she said. "George. I like it."

"Miranda," I said. "My name is pretty much the only thing I didn't leave behind."

She laughed.

"There's a, um, topless beach, off that way, a mile or so through the Navy Base. If you'd like to join me..."

"Any direction he isn't going is fine with me," said George, gesturing with a shoulder after the Man Mountain.

I laughed and nodded. "The topless thing is optional, of course. Topoptional."

"Toptional," said George. "I'm very very pale," she said. "It would be bad to get sunburned."

"It is bad to get your boobs sunburned," I said. There, we had a word for them, right here in our little conversation. "I can tell you this from experience. I heartily don't recommend it."

We found a shady spot under a tree to spread out our towels, and at least while we were there, George followed my example. She covered up for the occasional brief dip in the waves. On the Cuban side of the island there's actually a little surf. Except if there's a hurricane. Then there's a lot of surf and you don't want to be anywhere near the place.

"You have plans for dinner?" George asked, after a delightful afternoon.

"Nope. Day off. I am a free woman," I told her.

"What's good here?" she asked.

"Depends on the budget, but..."

"You may indulge yourself," she said. "I always wanted to say that."

We went to her B&B, where she insisted I come in to her tiny room while she changed. And then we went to my almost equally tiny apartment, where I returned the favor. It was... racy. Thing about changing out of your bathing suit is you're naked, in a tiny apartment, with another girl right there. And then you put on a minidress and only feel a little less naked, for her, at least.

And then we went to the spot on the harbor and scored a table where we could watch the sun set. They brought us Cuban coffee and a little charcoal grill thing for the table so we could do our tuna in pieces, and eat it hot off the fire. And I took her to Rum Runners, where we got smashed, and then home again. At least her place had a queen sized bed.

I felt a little self-conscious, waking up next to this chick whose name I didn't even know, watching her bed head figure out which side her face was on, paw itself open and then look at me, squinting. "What was that stuff we drank last night?"

"Rum," I said. "I think. I remember going in..."

"And then we..." she said. By this time she was sitting up against the far wall, knees up under the blanket, but those amazing boobs were punctuating her gestures.

"Apparently so," I said. "I'd love to say I remember every moment and you were fabulous, but I really don't."

"Yeah that," she said. "You're actually a girl," she said.

"I am actually a girl," I confirmed.

"I, uh," she said. "Huh."

"What happens in Key West stays in Key West," I quoted. It's kind of remarkable how many of the tourists on the boat say that. "It's okay, both of my moms are lesbians, I come by it honestly."

"Both... moms..."

"And I have blown your mind," I said. "What a rude way to wake up in the morning. It's like *Hey, gmorning*, and *Pffft!* Mind blown."

"And me without my... much of anything at all," she said, dropping the pretense of modesty. "I should write that down. If I had a pen. And a card. And a pocket or something."

"If I had a pen, I would write it down, if I had a notebook," I suggested.

"Yeah. You should be a poet," said George. "Or an editor."

"I'm just a lifeguard on a tourboat," I said.

"You are not *just* anything at all. I've seen your scars, how you put yourself together again and came here to the end of the road," said George.

"You're here, too," I said. "And can we have the philosophy later when I'm not hung over?"

"Deal. Orange juice will fix you up." And she put on yesterday's dress and went out on the verandah with a dozen tourists to fetch it. I was still trying to remember how to tie myself into mine. Somehow it came all apart last night. Normally I keep it on a hangar, kind of tied together, and you don't actually have to figure out which strap goes through what loop and meets another one around over there to make a nice, attractive bow, which makes the whole thing actually look like a dress when it's totally not. Um, that made sense in my head.

"Are you working today?" she asked.

"Yeah. I should go. Help me figure this thing out." Which she did. First opening a curtain or two, not minding if she shared naked me with the town. The light was helpful. "Dinner again tonight?"

"I'd love to," I said.

And I dreamed of her all day, while kayaking and snorkeling with random pink tourists. And making a different big ex-Marine shave his mustache so his snorkeling mask wouldn't leak. That's always such fun.

Chapter Seventeen

Ravynscroft

Lia 2014

It's a long train ride, through the dark. I chatted with my seat mate til she got off in Philly. Then I went looking for food. "Where's home?" I asked the person in the dining car. It was kind of a snack bar with a microwave and prepackaged meals of various kinds.

"New York," she said. "I go off shift in two hours."

"Long day," I said.

She looked at me, nodding. "You okay, honey?" she asked.

And the answer is no, but you don't say that to strangers. I sat down on one of the stools to eat my wrap sandwich, and chatted with her when she wasn't busy.

I slept for a while after New York. The snack bar wouldn't be the same with somebody different running it. There are a bunch of stops in, Connecticut it must be, where there's a complicated spiel they read out over the intercom about how the train is longer than the platform so please don't try to exit through doors that aren't open. About the fourth time through I figured out what they were talking about.

It was like eight in the morning when the train pulled into the station in Boston. You find your luggage, get out of the train onto these long concrete platforms between the tracks, and walk toward the station. Rachael was standing just outside the doors, looking at the crowd. I was right next to the locomotive, still idling loudly, when she ran up to me for a hug. She took my suitcase and we went indoors.

There were tables all around the big room, and fast food dealers around the edges, in the next room, and a couple out on the floor itself. Rachael steered me toward a table with five chairs, which three women were managing to occupy.

"Hey, guys, I found her," said Rachael.

Everybody stood up.

"This is Ravyn, my ex," said Rachael.

"Welcome," said Ravyn. She's shorter than I am and has lots of very curly hair. She pushed some of it out of her face, flipping it over a shoulder. Rachael divested me of my backpack, and I felt like I might float away, so I embraced Ravyn to help weight me down.

"Andi," said Andi. She's a bit taller, with spiky blonde hair. "I'm the blonde one," she said.

"I can see that," seemed the thing to say at the time.

"And this is Joy," said Rachael. Wild red curls were cut short enough to manage, unlike Ravyn's black hair which is nearly as curly.

"Hi," said Joy.

Ravyn said, "The other member of our..."

"gang," said Joy.

"...is actually in the bathroom at the moment," said Ravyn.

"Bathroom. What a great idea," I said. So Rachael took me there.

"JJ, meet Lia," Rachael said to a short Asian woman who was leaving as we entered.

"Pleasure," said JJ.

"Likewise," I said.

"There will be a quiz when we get back to the table," said Rachael.

"It's all kind of overwhelming," I admitted.

"They don't bite," said Rachael. "Unless you ask nicely."

She made me laugh. It was fun. I couldn't remember the last time I'd had simple fun.

They found me some breakfast, which was also welcome. "Hokay," said JJ. "We should take you home."

"Home," I said, kind of wistfully.

"Aw, honey, don't cry," Rachael said, with her arm around my shoulders. "We'll take good care of you."

"So there's a subway; it's probably a lot like the one you have in DC," said Ravyn. "We have an extra Charlie card, and put some cash on it. You use it at the turnstiles."

"Charlie on the MTA," I sang, on cue. "The Metro just came to Tysons Corner last year. And now we don't live there any more to use it."

"Yeah, exactly. Here's the map of the system," said Ravyn, stopping me on the platform facing the obligatory abstract map of the city, showing, pretty much, only the subway stops and connections. "We live near Oak Grove. Right now we're at South Station."

"So we get the Red train to, um," I said, crouching down and tilting my head so the bifocals would let me read. "Downtown Crossing. And then the Orange one to Oak Grove."

"Exactly. You pass this quiz," she said, and we laughed.

So we did that, and they let me navigate, with only a little bit of a hint about changing trains. "I suppose you get used to the underground stations and how they stack," I said.

JJ happened to be nearby when I said that, so she nodded. "You'll get the hang of it."

The sun was in my eye when we came out of the tunnel. But we arrived safely at the end of the line. Upstairs to the station so we could cross over the tracks, and down to the parking lot. Andi popped open the trunk and we stowed my stuff. The car was not quite big enough for six adults, but most of them are small, so we squeezed in.

"So, I'm sure you're wondering," said Rachael. "So I'll just babble for a while and everybody can be embarrassed and nobody has to say anything. Ravyn and I met in grad school, actually not so very long after I got dumped by Becca and Stephan, whom you know."

"They lived next door to us in Virginia," I said. "And you came to visit, which is where I met you."

"Right. It was a fun trip," said Rachael. "We got married, Ravyn and I, found a house in the suburbs with a picket fence, started working on the 2.3 kids thing and discovered we were lesbians and there was something missing..."

I was laughing. I mean, of course they knew. But that's what Rachael was angling for, and she was a great story teller. "Ah, right. Massachusetts. You can actually get married here."

"Then comes the sad part. *Never fall in love with a bisexual woman,* the lesbians will tell you," said Rachael.

"I've heard that," I said.

"Well, it turns out there are men out there who make me go all puppy-eyed."

"So she moved out," said Ravyn. "Blah blah blah lots of sad stuff including way too many hookups with your ex, and..."

"And I needed a place to stay what with my lease expiring," said JJ, "so Ravyn invited me to move in. And, um, stuff."

"And me," said Andi. "More or less the same story."

"And, um, stuff," said Ravyn. She was smiling.

"And then they were talking a little too loudly in a bar about how great it was to have a house full of lesbians to go home to every night, and I started to cry," said Joy. "They're great, and so now there are four of us."

"You..." I said.

"All sleep together, yes," said Ravyn, quickly.

"I was gonna say *fuck*," said Joy.

"I know you were," said Ravyn.

"This is like watching a tennis match," I said. "You finish each other's..."

"Sentences," said JJ.

And so we laughed again. They do a lot of laughing.

"So four women, three beds, it's all kinds of wonderful," said Ravyn. "Reminds me of being the dormgirl."

"I, uh, don't know what to say," I said. The honest truth, for once.

"We can survive on two bedrooms, I'm sure," said Ravyn, looking at her housemates. "So you get one of your own, if you want. No pressure."

"Thank you," I said. "I've always been... sort of..."

"Monogamous," said Joy. "What's up with that?"

"I was gonna say *boring*, but you got it," I said to Joy. "And my life is kinda complicated right now without..."

"Fucking wenches," said Joy.

"Yeah," I said. Not looking at Joy this time, or anybody else, fascinated by the way my hands seemed to be wrestling in my lap.

"As I said, no pressure," said Ravyn. "You're our guest. You can stay as long as you need to."

"Thank you," I said. "You guys are life savers."

"You wanna stay for lunch, Raitch?" Ravyn asked.

"I'd like that," said Rachael. "I feel kinda responsible..."

"Becca is very persuasive, as you know," said Ravyn. They laughed together, nodding, "It seems like every time she came to visit she left a homeless person behind, to stay with us for a couple days."

"When I used to live here," said Rachael.

"You're still around pretty often," said JJ. "And speaking for myself, you're welcome here."

The other three voting members of the household nodded agreement.

"It's almost like you're a religious order," I said.

"You're not the first person to say that," said JJ. "My... ahem," and she looked at Joy.

"Barrista?" said Joy.

"She said we were the Little Sisters of the Holy Fuck," said JJ, blushing.

You just have to laugh sometimes, so I did. It actually is funny, once you wrap your head around how serious it is. "It's... an odd situation, but it seems to be working for you."

"Yes," said Ravyn. "And yes, it does seem to work. It's so different from the dreams we had as kids. You have to let some things go, but it's pretty good."

Chapter Eighteen

Real Life in Paradise

Miranda 2015

Eventually the vacation ended and George decided not to go back to... whatever it was she had come to the end of the road trying to leave behind. So we had a little chat and she moved into my little apartment, and we were really chummy. They say two can live as cheaply as one, and it was certainly way cheaper than her being in a B&B, but not as cheap as me living there alone. So she canvassed the businesses and came home smiling.

"What are you grinning at?" I asked. "I mean besides me changing out of my work bathing suit."

"You are looking at an employed woman."

Actually, I was looking at my closet, trying to pick out something lightweight for the evening of... well, eating in, because we really couldn't afford eating out very much. But I turned to look at my newly employed... um, partner, I guess she is. "Wow. Congratulations! Where?"

"That funky butterfly museum? They wanted help running the gift shop. I can do retail," said George.

"Coool," I said. "You rock."

"So..." she said, later, over boiled shrimp. Hey, it was cheap at the fish market, and even I can successfully boil stuff. And once you learn what funny peppers to put in the cocktail sauce, that's cheap, too. Mom would be so proud. Lia, we're calling her.

"So?" I prompted.

"It's really okay if I stay here?" she asked.

"It's really okay. In fact I like having you around. And, um, stuff." My eye stole a glance at the bed. "It would help, of course, if you can help out with the rent and food and things."

"Of course," said George. "And while I really do like being called George, I should probably tell you my actual name is Constance Johnson. Just in case somebody asks you if you know her."

"Con, then," I said. "Or Connie? If you insist on a more feminine form."

She shuddered visibly.

"I could always call you George when you wanna be the boy."

Chapter Nineteen

Somebody needs to tell this

Mo 2014

OK, so somebody is going to have to tell this part of the story, now that Lia and Miranda have gone off in opposite directions. Sarah's not that much of a story teller. Orally, sure. Getting her to write brings up flashbacks of proposals and peer review and gives her the heebie jeebies.

I'm Mo Grant. I'm a transexual. When I was in high school, I was Maurice. Lia's told her version of all that. And we'll get to... other witnesses, as the more recent Bible translations put it in their footnotes. Yeah, I read the fine print. It keeps you alive sometimes.

After high school, at the urging of my dad and the assistant principal, I signed up for the Marines. It was arguably the biggest mistake of my life, but it certainly changed everything. They said it would make a man of me. It did help me find the courage to become a woman.

Anyway, every vet has stories that will curl your hair, and I'm not going to tell them. I got training as a combat medic. Everybody in the Marines is an infantry person first, so there's that, too. After a couple of reenlistments, I decided not to fight it any more, and walked away. And found out how awful life can be for vets, especially if they're wounded. You'd think the war machine would take care of its own, and they certainly told us it does, but the VA is due for a revolution real soon, and they've been training the malcontents to be able to do it. They just need an organizer.

Mama Mo, the woman who knows what they're suffering because she's been there. There's no money in it, but hey, most of the vets I see are either in VA facilities that are falling down around their ears, or they're homeless, and I'm better off than that. I share what I have, and somehow there's always more.

Yes, I'm coming back to Lia's family story. Let's start with getting to know Sarah. I first met her at Liz's funeral. She seems a solid, bookish geeky kind of a person, which works well with what she does: study the actual workings of fertility from the molecular level to the actual (there's that word again) making of real live babies. But there's also something defiant in her eye. She's somebody I would have been proud to go into combat with, I think. They told her she couldn't have kids of her own, so she spent 20 years figuring out how to prove them wrong.

"Work hard, do your homework, cheat a little when you have to," is something she would quote pretty often. And so there's some kind of family secret we all respect. Everybody's got them, I suppose, and your friends know what questions not to ask. Making Miranda and Susie was unethical, pretty clearly, and maybe illegal, but there they are, growing up happy and healthy.

Until they got smashed because their parents are queer, and Northern Virginia is still kicking and screaming about being dragged into the 20th century, let alone the 21st.

Anyway, Liz. I poked around some, with Cris, because it's always suspicious when somebody you know is queer gets offed before her time. But apparently it really was an accident. Sailing, swimming off the boat, companion got into trouble, Liz rescued her, but got tired and didn't make it herself. It's sad, but it happens.

It was good getting to know Cris again, and Sarah had really good taste in whiskey, so we took her up on the offer to keep in touch.

I forget where Lia was, but Sarah and I were in a bar, waiting for Cris, and she wanted more details about the Misfit Toys, what we called ourselves when we were in high school together.

"What's to say. We kind of started hanging out with each other. Nobody was out about much of anything, even to ourselves, but I think we sensed that we were all acting, trying to look normal on the outside, hiding some great secret. I was kind of a wimpy guy with hair longer than boys wore it then. Cris was pretty butch, and we really did look kind of alike in some ways. Lia was... pretending to be the average geeky science nerd but there was something about the desperation in her eyes that attracted us to her. And Liz... Well, Liz took no nonsense from anybody. Her dad apparently told her whopping lies all the time, fantastical stories, so she came by it honestly, but she could stare you right in the eyes and tell you day was night and black was white and you'd implicitly believe her. She was a good nucleus for a group of closeted queer kids. Though *closeted* kind of implies we knew what we were, and we just knew something was wrong without knowing what."

"Tell me about the football team," said Sarah.

"They were in my gym class. They went everywhere together, they weighed 250 or more each, the offensive line. I think when we were alone together we joked that they really were offensive, but you didn't dare do anything within earshot of them. They beat me up because they could, because I wouldn't fight back, because I was a wimp, and ultimately because I'm transgendered, I think, though none of us could have found words for that then." I had to pause, remembering what being a frightened kid was like.

"Chris made me come to karate with her. I learned a few things, but it wasn't enough. I learned a lot more later in the Marines."

"There was some kind of a fight," Sarah prompted.

"Yeah. We did pizza night at Delmonico's, the four of us, every month or so. I think Liz was trying to teach Lia to lie effectively, and all she managed to do was to get Lia to admit she had crushes on everybody at the table, and that therefore she must be gay, or bi, or something, and that she hated talking about herself. Cris pointed out she didn't have to talk about her sex life, but Lia thought that was pretty much the only thing worth lying about. She sucked at keeping secrets."

Sarah laughed and nodded.

"Anyway, we almost literally ran into the football team in the alley outside Delmonico's. You've seen the place, you can imagine the tactical situation. It's narrow enough that the five of them, side by side like they were on the football field, could block the alley. They were dissing my hair and our androgyny and Cris was about to strike so I stepped in and got flattened. I dunno what-all else happened, exactly, except later there were cops and Lia was mostly out of her dress and then even later everything magically evaporated. We got detention at school, once we all returned, but the football guys didn't. Or maybe it happened while we were being patched up."

"Oh. Here's Cris," said Sarah.

Chapter Twenty

Chris' Tale

Mo 2014

Cris came in, quietly confident, and sat down. I smiled at Cris and let him.. them... whatever she is today... dominate the conversation.

"Hi," said Sarah.

"Hey," said Cris. The motorcycle leather jacket was unzipped, gloves tucked into the side pocket. A booted foot rested on the rung of the next chair over. Cris was the picture of relaxation.

Sarah was nervous, sitting straight in her chair, and despite the slacks she was wearing, her knees were close together. "Can I ask you something?"

"You can ask," said Cris, with a small hint of a smile.

"What happened to you guys... The misfits, I mean."

"Misfit Toys," said Cris. "Somebody got that out of a Christmas movie when we were kids."

"I remember the Burl Ives snowman."

"That's the one, yeah," said Cris.

There was a long silence. Cris was examining Sarah closely.

"Two questions for you, first," said Cris.

"Sure," said Sarah.

"One, what is it you want to know? And two, do you even want to know?"

"Well, Lia has this construction that strikes me as teenage bullshit, involving cardboard cutouts of football players, only one of whom has any personality."

"James. He was the center."

"Yeah. And Mo says he laid into you pretty hard."

"She says that? Huh," said Cris. She glanced at me with a tiny smile on his lips.

"Huh?"

"A lot of stuff happened that night. I'm not surprised Lia's version is... edited." Cris thought for a while, looking at Sarah's face.

Sarah was obviously trying to hold very still, wondering what she was telling us nonverbally.

"Sanitized, perhaps," said Cris.

"As you said the other night," Sarah started.

"At Liz's funeral."

"Yeah. Lia's remarkably good at self-editing."

"She always was. Sometimes for one reason, sometimes for another," said Cris. "The fact that you are aware of that probably bodes well for your relationship with her."

"I'm beginning to appreciate just how deep the subterfuges go," said Sarah. "So I guess I do want to know."

"Okay," said Cris. "Remember you asked."

Sarah nodded. Cris' eyes defocused, looking at something now far away and long ago.

~

Cris 1987

It was a hot summery night. We did pizza night, more or less in the usual way. At that same place we had your remarkably nice whiskey after the funeral.

To Liz.

Cris sipped.

Lia, the one member of the group who was remotely fashionable, had some kind of a multi-layered flyaway nothing of a mini sundress. I'm not a girl any more, I don't even know. Backless, but she wore it like it was painted on or something. I had a crush on that girl since we were in kindergarten, it seems like. I'm sure that's wrong. Probably fifth grade, though. Cute little purse between her arm and her boob. I mean, hubba hubba. But we were in high school so of course I didn't do anything. She let Liz maneuver her into confessing her undying love for her, Liz, though I'm pretty sure that glance at me meant something.

We went outside and the four of us ran into the five members of the football team, standing shoulder to shoulder like they always did. They picked on Mo like they owned him, and he just kinda let them do it. I had badgered him into taking karate with me, and he knew a few moves, but nothing you could take into a fight. James seemed a little offended somehow by the fact that Mo and I dressed alike and had the same hair.

So, yeah. Things got... dynamic. Lia stepped in between James and me just as he was about to strike. Curtis got a handful of fabric, which mercifully, at least from a tactical point of view, tore off in his hand. I remember her whirling to look at John, her hair coming undone and going everywhere. He was crouched like a lineman, ready to tackle or block or whatever the hell they do, between Lia and the only way out. Meanwhile Mo was getting beat up--again-- and Curtis, dropping what was left of Lia's dress turned to me.

Liz had the presence of mind to do the only sensible thing: run back into the restaurant and scream for help. I managed to connect with Curtis's crotch, and he went down. James came up behind Lia and ripped off the rest of her dress. I couldn't help her, and Mo was down by this time. I got Joe and Harry pretty good, but it wasn't enough. It'll never be enough. Mo still blames herself for not being the man that night. In a way I guess I do, too.

James and John, damn, they sound like apostles or something. Well, having a naked girl struggling between them, you know the rest, I imagine. Every girl's nightmare. I had wanted to see Lia's breasts since she had any, and I did, but I really didn't want it like that, at all.

Cops, ambulances. I think I blacked out. None of it makes any sense, but the next part makes even less. I didn't see Lia again for a while. I was in the hospital and rehab and psychiatrists' offices a lot, and hardly ever at school. Liz came to visit pretty often, and I think I told her a whole lot more than I ever did my shrink. About being done with the whole girl thing, while at the same time not wanting anything to do with men--either being one or being around them. Except Mo, who cried out loud every time I saw him.

Lia talked at first, about all the doctors and the cops and the men who spread her legs and stared and took samples and raped her all over again with the legal niceties of their investigation. And then somehow everything magically went away. Maybe because we were so traumatized we couldn't testify. Or something. Maybe because James' dad was the DA.

We were more or less patched up by the time school started in the fall. The linemen were still playing football, just like before. I refused to go to pep rallies and games; dropped out of gym class. Dropped out of gender, truth to tell. We struggled through our senior year. Lia managed to catch up. She shut up about the trauma, and nobody wanted to push. We all knew from our own experience how hard it is, how individual recovery is, and so we just hung out and were friends, without pushing each other in any way. Dunno if that was helpful or not.

Mo went off to the Marines as soon as he was old enough, pushed by that bastard assistant principal, and by his dad, who was also a bastard. I... managed. Lived on the streets for a long time, wrestled my demons to the end of the round, at least. Bounced for a while. There's some kind of advantage, when you're throwing a drunk out of a bar, if he doesn't know whether you're a girl or a boy. Keep him guessing. And my steel-toed boots found more than one crotch. It's kind of amazing watching tough guys crumple.

Apparently Lia just forgot the whole thing. I think for most of our senior year, she carefully didn't talk about it, until it was just edited out of her life and her memory. Can't say that's wrong; it's not my way, but it's a way of coping. If it works for her, great.

Chapter
Twenty-One

The Conspiracy

Mo 2014

Anyway. That's just background. The three of us, Cris, Sarah, and I, hit it off pretty well.

And then Miranda had her... accident. We're all calling it an accident. This kid Sam had been harassing her in school, so Sarah asked if I could kind of keep an eye on them, Miranda and Sam, and keep them apart. And I almost did, dammit. Vicky asked Miranda out to coffee, how romantic. And then coming out of the shop... does this sound familiar? Sam ran her down with his dad's car.

Combat medic training kicked in, and even though I was too late to prevent the accident, I could help the victim. I checked vitals, found several broken bones and a head injury, and lay down on top of her to hold her still, screaming for Vicky or somebody else to call 911. Which Vicky did, but only after she had snapped pictures of the license plate.

The ambulance was there pretty quickly, and they let me ride along, in part I think because I could sling medical jargon with the best of them. They taped her to a backboard and hoisted her into the ambulance. I remember waving to Vicky as they shut the door and we drove off.

So I called Sarah, and I called Lia, and I was in the waiting room when they arrived. Lia had a briefcase and a determined look in her eye that reminded me of a wounded grizzly bear more than anything else. She started going through documents, living wills, and more, with the guy at the counter, who wondered why all this was happening to him. Sarah pulled out her GW Hospital badge that said "Dr Hartley" on it, and that was good enough for him.

I guess it was touch and go back in the back, but eventually they came through again, bound for another ambulance and a transfer to GW across the river.

"Where to?" I asked Lia.

"I'm going too," she said.

"I'm driving," I insisted, and she gave me her keys. She shuffled papers in the passenger seat, putting the legal paperwork back in order again.

Hours later, Sarah emerged, sweaty and tired, and said, "She's stable. Had to push way more steroids than anybody could believe to get her brain to stop swelling. And she's in a medical coma for a while. So we'll see."

Lia relaxed. And then her phone tweeted. The day was not over yet. It was the neighbor lady, Becca Grossman. Lia put it on the speaker so Sarah could hear.

"I'm so sorry," Becca was saying. She wasn't crying, exactly, but her voice was wobbling. "I didn't know Susie was home alone. The guy from the school system you told me about? The gatherer of information. He came back with a sheriff or something, so I let them borrow my house key when they couldn't get an answer. The cop said you were unfit parents and made some comments about gay this and that."

"Where's Susie? Oh God, where's Susie?" Lia wailed.

"State custody, apparently," said Becca. "That has to be the fastest unfit parent finding in the history of bureaucracy. Just for the record, you guys are as fit as any parents I know, and I'll testify to that in court if you need me to."

"Thanks," said Sarah. "I, uh, don't know what to do."

"Me, neither," said Lia.

"Let me... see what I can do," I suggested, already thumbing through my mental rolodex of people who know people who can find out things.

"Just this morning, life was pretty good," Lia said when the phone call was over. "Went off to work in the usual way, kissed the wife and kids goodbye. And now? One kid is in a coma, the other one's in state custody, the wife is... dead tired and if she blames me I can understand it."

I found a social worker at the hospital, who told me they have a dorm like thing with apartments for families of patients to stay in. She arranged a room for Lia and Sarah, and I left them there, taking the subway back to Tysons Corner.

There are a lot of homeless vets around who know things, can find things out, and I put the word out that we needed to know what happened to Susie. Word spreads quickly about these things.

Chapter Twenty-Two

Beginnings

Mo 2014

Cris and I are kind of like peas in a pod, except we're complete opposites. When we were in high school, Cris was a girl and I was a boy. Then I was a man for a while. Now I'm a woman. Is Marine a gender? I was that for a while, too. Now, I'm a vet. Cris gave up on femininity, and I think that if men and women can't understand each other, M2F and F2M transpeople have even less chance. But Cris is more F2x or something. Anything not female, he says. Not male either, she says.

With Liz gone, Cris moved to the Northern Virginia burbs. It's a bigger city environment, easier to lose yourself in the underworld, and so, maybe, safer for queer people.

But I still love picking his brain, whenever she's up for it. Conspiracy theories roll so naturally off his tongue, and she's involved in half of them. Stirring things up. My network of discharged wounded vets could be... useful.

Charlie is a guy who wanders around, mostly invisible, asking questions you forget as soon as he walks away. I found him in Walter Reed, in a shithole of a room with paint peeling off the ceiling. He has PTSD, I mean, who doesn't? They give you a weapon and you kill people with it and they're trying to kill you and all you really want is to go home to your mommy. And they let you do that, but it's not home anymore, because you're not you anymore.

So when Aunt Mo comes around, speaking your language, sharing war stories toe to toe, knowing when to shut up and listen? Stuff happens and it's not anything the VA did. You may not end up employable or even off the streets, but there's a club out there that's got your back, and that's something.

So when the DA sends the cops out to clear the streets, they don't win friends or influence the people who matter, the grit on the sandpaper, where the real heavy lifting of civilization is done.

Joe, good old GI Joe, he was the one Army guy. So we'd go *Semper Fi* and he'd be all you what now? But man can he walk point.

And they all thought it was kinda funny that the old Gunny is a woman now, but like, shrug, whatever. We all know life is really bad sometimes, and you do what you need to do.

So Cris and I, we kinda figured maybe we could stage a rerun of Misfit Toys vs. the Football Team, this time with more toys and less grunts. Explain that, well, we don't like your kind around here, on the streets. So you give us Susie and we...

"We don't hurt you, too much," said Cris.

Yeah, that's the best thing we could come up with.

So we looked up Sarah. We'd ask Lia, but she's... written the Toys out of her life, for one thing. And will believe anything she needs to. Which, who am I to judge? But it's not the kind of thing you need in a situation. Sarah's pretty solid, though. I learned that in the emergency room that night when we brought Miranda in.

"Lia still has the dress," was Sarah's first comment.

"The dress." I said. It's a Marine thing. You repeat something when you're confused.

"She had this thing she kept in a garment bag in the back of her closet, since I met her. Kind of like the memories," said Sarah. "Edited, sanitized, protected from real life. I looked at it once; it's a purple backless flyaway summer sundress, that matches the descriptions you two gave me. Oh, and it's torn. Carefully preserved, held together enough to hang up in a closet, but otherwise useless."

"Until now," said Cris.

"Until now," said Sarah. "We can inspect it for stains and... well, DNA sequencing is cheap nowadays."

"I am having an idea," I said to Cris.

"Me too," said Cris to me.

"We'll need some samples to compare to."

We both looked at Sarah like, "Riiiight, how are we going to..."

"Saliva is easy. Hair with follicles will also do," said Sarah.

"Hmmm... I wonder if Charlie..." I said.

"Just kinda pocket a drinking glass," said Cris.

"Oh, hey, he eats at my restaurant a lot," I said. "Duh."

"Think, Mo," said Cris, grinning. "That's what you're good at."

"I'm sure the statute of limitations has expired," said Sarah.

"But this is the court of public opinion," I said. "He's running for re-election. He doesn't need a youthful indiscretion (not to mention class one felony) to come up just now."

"How do we do that?" Sarah asked.

"There's this guy I knew, Dweezil, we called him... Wrote for *Stars and Stripes* in the Corps." I thought for a while. "I'm pretty sure he's around someplace. I saw him in Walter Reed a few times. Charlie knows these things. Keeps track of people. I should ask Charlie."

Chapter Twenty-Three

To Old Times

Mo 2014

From time to time two or three of the old offensive linemen would get together. Dinner, coffee, maybe a drink. It was rare that all five were in the same town at the same time, so this was special. The bar and grill where I worked was funky; it was much less antiseptic than the glass and steel downtown area. It kind of reminded them of where they grew up, playing football together outside Winchester. Way outside Winchester.

James took the opportunity to observe as the guys drifted in. Curtis came first; he was still really big. They were all tall, but some had kept the weight and turned it into fat, while others, John for example, had slimmed down and adapted to office jobs of one kind or another.

"Beer," said Curtis. "Whaddya got?"

I recognized James, and gave his buddies some latitude because James tipped well. I rattled off the beer list.

"Bud," said Curtis.

"What are you, a redneck?" laughed John, ordering the local microbrew.

"Bud Lite," said Curtis. "Gotta watch my weight."

"Watch it go higher and higher," said Harry, taking a seat.

Harry was not a small man himself. "Where's Joe?"

"Stuck in traffic, I imagine," said James.

"Well, this is wrong," said Joe, arriving as if on cue. "James was the center, so he needs to be in the middle, with John and me on his right and Harry and Curtis on his left."

"Everything in just that order," said James, smiling. "The table's round, so you'll have to sit next to Curtis," he pointed out.

"I'll live, I imagine," said Joe. "The signboards on the interstate seemed to be bored; they were flashing poems."

"Seems like it would be distracting," James said.

"Only if you can read," said Curtis, and everyone laughed.

"It is thanks to poetry that I am more or less sane," said Joe. "It's kind of like football: say something artfully, with no wasted words or motions. Knock some sense into the guy across the line, and still be standing for the next one coming at you."

"Did that make sense to you?" asked John.

"Not really," said James.

"Good," said John. "I was a little worried I'd missed the signal."

"GREEN. FORTY-FIVE. OMAHA!" shouted Curtis from across the table.

And James and John separated as if by instinct, waiting for a halfback to try to carry the ball between them. Old habits die hard.

I took the cue and placed myself in the gap. "My name is Mo and I'll be your server tonight," I said. I told them about the specials, and took a few more drink orders.

"You..." said Curtis, looking me up and down. "You remind me of somebody."

"I get that a lot. You boys ready to order? Or I can give you a few minutes." I wandered away. The place wasn't busy, so I wasn't out of earshot.

They examined the menu more or less in silence until I returned.

"I don't know what I want," said Harry. "You start."

So they went around the table. "OK, Sport, your turn again," I said. And Harry had more or less decided.

"Sometimes I just open my mouth and whatever comes out is what I order," he said as I walked away.

"Always the talkative one," said Curtis. "I remember having to shut you up in the huddle sometimes."

"Fun times," said Joe, with a sigh. "So I hear you're running for re-election," he said.

"Yeah," said James. "Should be easy, but there's some flack about police action and stuff. It could get ugly. Football, now, was a game where you know the rules, and you bend them when you have to to keep your guy from getting through, but holding is just 10 yards and we go on to the next play."

"And everybody knew exactly why you had to do it," said John, "and the QB is happy you did, even if it complicates his life for the next couple plays. At least he still has a life."

"We all remember standing around feeling like hell when Bill O'Leary got his knee smashed and they had to take him off on a cart," said Harry.

I delivered the food, great steaming platters, almost completely covering the table. Conversation was replaced by the sounds of feasting.

"Remember that pizza joint..." said John, smearing butter on a roll. "Del somebody's"

"Delmonico's," said Harry.

"Yeah, that's it," said John. "The circular table in the corner, where we'd sit just like this and devour pie after pie."

"With the little people in the opposite corner, talking about... whatever it is that queers talk about, I guess," said James.

"So, James," said John. "They tell me the way to win elections is to distract the voters from the actual issues."

"I hear that," said James. "It's a little hard at the local level; people know what the DA does or doesn't do."

"Nah," said John. "Nobody's paying that much attention unless you lose a big case. Just bust some queers and it taps into everybody's yuck factor. Think of the children. That kind of thing."

"Could work," said James. "Can I have some of that butter?"

"Oh hey," said Harry. "There's a really interesting case in the schools. You might like this."

"Most school stuff doesn't really rise to the level of prosecution," said James.

"Girl gets into a fight at the high school. There's a couple split lips, broken glasses, no real harm done. We investigate; there's forms to fill out. All the blanks, they keep telling me."

"Yeah, I have to keep sending stuff back to the cops for that," said James.

"Anyway," said Harry, "The parentage of this girl is... odd. She's living with these two ladies, and her sister who's, oh, seven or so. Maybe ten. And I figure the one is the mom, and we fill that in. She won't tell me who the father is. It happens. But she insists the other lady is also a parent. Name on the birth certificate, she says."

"Huh."

"And we have that on file at the school system, so I pull it, and sure enough. It comes from Maryland or the District or something, but it's a birth certificate, and I got another copy just to be sure it's legit, and there we go: the two parents are named Sarah and Lia."

"Wasn't there a Lia in our high school?" asked John.

"I hadn't thought of that, but I bet it's her," said Harry. "Women, uh, age poorly sometimes. Especially when there are kids."

Rueful shaking of heads went around the table, remembering the shapely cheerleader types most of them had married, becoming middle-aged moms. Of course they were no prime specimens themselves, but that came on gradually and they didn't notice most of the time.

"Anyway," Harry said again. "Same kid gets whacked by a car, possibly driven by the same boy she had fists with in school."

James sat up.

"Right about the time we were doing a surprise home visit to check on fitness and all that," said Harry.

"And the kid was taken to the hospital here, but got spirited away across the river before she was even stable, to hear the nurses tell it. My Janie is a nurse in the ER. Oh and the kid sister? She was home alone. So of course that's not a fit household."

"Perfect messy situation for some politicking," said John.

"Ain't it, though?" said Harry. "If I were you, I'd love me," he told James. "You can maybe bust the other lady for kidnapping, open up that can of worms. See what crawls out."

"Can I get you boys any dessert?" I was asking, as I stacked a number of plates and dishes on my other arm. "The pecan pie is to die for."

"Sure," said Curtis. He patted his soft belly.

"Five slices," said John.

"More beer?" I asked.

"Sure."

So I was within earshot, one fist wrapped around five beer mugs and the other supporting a tray of plates of pie.

"This could really work," said James. "John, you're my campaign manager, would you get up with Harry and sort out the details, figure out what we can do with it?"

"I can smell blood in the water," said John.

"Lawyers," said Curtis, with a snort.

"To old times," said James, holding up his beer mug. Four others clicked against it.

I made a point of bussing the table myself, and bagging and labeling the water glasses they'd used. You never know when something might be useful...

Chapter Twenty-Four

How... Amazing

Lia 2015

So, yeah. They gave me a room of my own. For, like, the first time ever since I was a grad student. I've been listening to Sarah snore every night for... what, twenty years now.

"The doors..." said Ravyn.

"Don't latch," said JJ.

"Yours kinda almost does," said Rachael. "And I don't live here, I should go home."

"Thanks for coming by," said Ravyn. They walked to the door together, these one-time legally married women. I think I heard kissing.

"Hurry back," said Ravyn, closing the door. She was smiling when she rejoined us.

"How... very odd, being part of an *us,* not involving Sarah," I mused aloud. Talking to yourself out loud is not a normal kind of a thing to do. "And with way more than two of us in it. Five, if I count as one. Who, um, like..."

"Fuck," said Joy.

"Sleep together," said Andi. She put out her tongue at Joy.

"Somebody has to say all the naughty words," said JJ, grinning.

"Can I..." I said, feeling suddenly shy. "like..."

"Sure," said Ravyn.

"Have a rain check?" I said.

"Of course," said JJ. "Consent is sexy. Coercion, however subtle, really isn't."

"Thank you. You're sure I can have a room of my own?"

"Of course," said Ravyn.

"Thank you," I said again.

"Bedtime. Before you say thank you again," said Ravyn, holding up a finger and smiling at me. "There are towels in your room. You need anything else?"

"I don't think so," I said.

"We're not far away," said Ravyn, and she showed me how to use my hip to make the door latch.

And so there I was, in the silence, very tired, missing Sarah, missing Miranda, missing Susie most of all. Wondering, despite myself, what my hostesses were up to in the other bedrooms, and, frankly, coming up mostly empty.

I could remember a time when Sarah and I blew each other's minds, spending hours thinking up creative things to do with each other in bed. And then we turned into adults with a mortgage and two kids, two careers, secrets, lives to manage.

We were doing okay, mostly, until.

Well, okay, but without any safety net, it turns out. The ones we'd carefully constructed were somewhat helpful. The papers naming each other health care proxies for both kids did help a little in the ER. But ultimately it was her *Sarah Hartley, MD* badge from GW Hospital that did the trick.

The tears when they came were not so much missing the family as feeling sorry for myself, for the innate cussedness of the very straight world and how being female and queer and... well, the kids are illegal aliens, kinda sorta. Human, true, and born in the USA, so they're citizens. But conceiving them was certainly unethical and I'm sure a smart prosecutor could come up with multiple crimes we could be charged with.

I woke up several times in the night wondering where I was, remembering trying to sleep on the train, and settling into the lesbian safety net for another few hours' nap.

It was light when I startled awake. So I found a shirt and jeans and opened the bedroom door. To see Ravyn and JJ spooned together, asleep, in the room to my right. And Andi and Joy, doing something that made me want to turn the picture upside down to see if it made any more sense that way. I left them to their devices, and went in search of coffee.

"Oh, oops," said Andi, a few minutes later, standing naked in the doorway. "Sorry."

"What?" said Joy, running into her. "Oh. Sorry."

And they scampered to the bathroom, which in this odd house is off the kitchen, so you have to go either through the kitchen or the dining room to get from the bedrooms to the bathroom.

I was still grinning when Ravyn and JJ appeared, duly clothed.

"What?" said JJ.

"Andi and Joy," I said, nodding toward the closed bathroom door. "Naked."

"Not unusual, I'm afraid," said Ravyn. "Especially on weekends."

"Weekends," I said. "I used to know what that means."

"Sorry your life has been upended," said Ravyn. "Let us know if there's anything we can do to help. And I do mean anything, pretty much."

"Than..."

"Hush," said Ravyn. "You need what we have. We're happy to share."

Andi and Joy popped open the bathroom door, and came through the kitchen, modestly (more or less) wrapped in their towels. I hated to interfere with the life of their household, but I did appreciate the accommodation.

We had fun that day, the five of us, doing Boston tourist things. "We never do the tourist attractions," said JJ.

"Only when we have an actual tourist with us," said Ravyn.

So we went to the Science Museum, and played with the exhibits and the demonstrations as only science professors can. They have a wide screen theater there, so to rest our feet we watched people climbing Everest in a storm. We went to the funky little museum at MIT, and saw whimsical machines built with handmade gears that do something trivial in complicated ways.

Chapter Twenty-Five

George

So here I was bopping along in high school, seventeen, kinda wondering what's up. And Sam, dear Sam, kinda backed me into a corner and I came out as gay. And it turns out my official BFF kissed me and I didn't even know she was gay. I didn't really know I was gay. And there we are, the poster couple for lesbian highschooldom. Which of course brings out the haters, like Sam.

And so I spent the rest of the school year in the hospital, watching my family fall apart. And when they let me out, all rehabbed and stuff, able to stand up all day and talk without getting too confused by the holes in my vocabulary... I found myself on the street after the moms split up, so I put out my thumb and in minutes was going south along the Interstate. Changed rides a couple times, ended up in Key West, at the end of the road. Well, for practical reasons, a few miles short of the end of the road, which is the high rent district. Lifeguarding off a boat, because, hey, I can swim like a fish, and we practiced that a lot when the walking thing wasn't really happening.

And a tourist came to town, and I caught her checking out my boobs, and she smiled. And she decided not to go home. Apartments are scarce, and we were sort of having a relationship, well, we were having relations at least, so she moved in. We need a bigger bed but there isn't room in the apartment, which is already like a third full of bed with just the twin one.

So there you have it. True Love. Or something. I should mention that George is a girl, in case you hadn't clued in yet. Because, hey, I told Sam I'm a lesbian, so whoever is waking up in my bed should be a girl.

Is that how it works? I don't even know. I've heard coming-out stories from the moms and their friends all my life, but somehow it was just stories until it happened to me. If that's what happened. Isn't it supposed to be, like, really really obvious to the person coming out? Not whether to come out; that's kind of subtle and I understand that. But whether there's something to be out about. I mean, sure, I'd always kinda been dreamy about both the girls and... well, some of the boys. Maybe.

Anyway, it's kind of habit forming, I guess, having somebody else living in your space. Not to mention the sex, which is also habit forming. It's hard to think straight when there's this sexy person in your life and you can't really get away even if you want, which you're not sure you do, because the apartment is tiny and it's pouring rain outside. Or not, but say it is.

Ohmygod thunderstorms, rolling up and down your spine and sometimes it seems like that palm tree that lost fronds across the street was our fault somehow. Or when the power goes out, because, you know, power surges and stuff.

We can do the boat thing without power, at least if there's a day's gas in it. George can't really do the gift shop thing, because cash registers are computers and even if the power comes up again they might have gotten fried. Because, you know, power surges and stuff.

Not to mention air conditioning, which is kinda necessary. So it was good to be going out on the water in my bathing suit that day. But damn if I wasn't having aftershocks, dreaming of George.

"You seem dreamy today," said the captain. Dez, she insisted I call her.

Last night's thunderstorm? I didn't say. My fault. "We're a little thin today," I said instead, looking at the tourists waiting to board. "Can I bring a friend? George's work is closed because of the power outage."

"Sure, why not," said Dez. And she went back to prepping the boat.

"George. Dock. Be here. Now." I texted.

"K sure. Am I bringing a bathing suit?"

"Yes. Skinny dipping is not a thing."

"Now you're smiling," said Dez.

And there was nothing I could say to that, either. I'm not telling my boss about fantasies of skinny dipping with my girlfriend off her boat.

Chapter Twenty-Six

Trading

Lia 2013

Susie. I'll try to remember.

It's hard to think with all these... attractive women in and out of the house all day long.

Susie. I'll try to remember.

In so many ways, she's just a kid, like any other. Less carefree, maybe, than Miranda was at her age? But you really can't compare them.

I remember one ordinary day, a while ago now, coming home from work. I parked the car in the driveway in the usual way, locked my keys inside, again, rang the bell, and there was Susie inside, checking to see who it was with the door on a chain, like we taught her. She closed the door again, fumbled with the chain for a while, and let me in. I gave her a hug, and she skipped off, back to whatever it is kids do after school. I should know, but I didn't.

Extra keys, unlock car, retrieve my own keys, briefcase, and the inevitable armload of stuff. Keys put away, the extras in the bowl in the mudroom, and mine in my purse. Right. Lose the jacket, hang it up. Drop purse and computer bag and briefcase in the office, check through all the stuff in my arms and sort it out like a letter carrier, delivering it to the right places.

Sarah blew through, went upstairs to change, and found Miranda upstairs in her room in tears. Teenagers. You know the drill. Actually, you don't, because it's different every time, but it's always the end of the world, somehow.

Susie was on the front steps, wearing her jacket because it was a little chilly. She brought home a friend. "Hi," I said.

"Hi," he replied.

"It's my Mama," Susie explained. "This is my friend Doug."

"Hi, Doug," I said.

"Hi, Mrs. Um, MacDonald," he said, looking to Susie for approval.

"So you guys are in school together," I guessed.

They nodded, grinning.

"Susie's never brought a boy home from school before," I said. It's hard to carry on a conversation with unresponsive kindergartners.

"I'm a girl," said Doug.

"Doug wanted to be a girl, and I was wondering what being a boy was like, so we traded," Susie announced, with a huge grin.

And somehow that made sense to me, as an adult, when the kids explained it. Gender is a thing of value; they had figured that out. And so you can't just change, you have to trade with somebody. Oh, to be six again. I put my hand over my mouth before I let myself smile.

"Susie's never brought home a girl from school before," I said, and Doug's grin was so big I thought he'd fall off the step. She would. English is hard. "Would you like to stay for supper?"

He... she... Doug... I guess he hadn't thought to come up with a feminine name... remembering his manners, said, "Yes, please."

"Tell me your last name? I'll call your mom and find out if it's okay."

Thankfully there was only one Siever on the list, so I called and it was fine. "I'm glad he's making friends," his mom told me.

"Yeah, me too, about Susie."

Change clothes. Right. Figure out what to cook. Sarah had the change thing done; I should learn from her example. So I went up the stairs and met her coming down.

"Can you talk some sense into Miranda? Nothing I say seems to help," she said.

"Sure. Find out what Doug will eat and what he wants for supper," I said.

"Who's Doug?" Sarah asked.

"Susie's friend. They're on the front steps. I called, he's staying for supper."

"Aha," said Sarah. "And Lia? I love you," she added, looking at the now open front of my blouse.

"I love you too?" I replied, pushing past her to get to the bedroom. Change clothes. Figure out Miranda. Somehow the first task was tractable and the second... it seemed a mountain to move, a labor of love to last all my life.

So, do the easy things first. Jeans. T-shirt, the green one with long sleeves. Pushed up halfway to the elbows. I tapped at Miranda's door and let myself in.

She was mostly done blubbering for the moment, and was busy blowing the resulting snot out of her nose.

"Mmm, snot," I said, and she laughed, despite the sob in her throat. The collision gave her the hiccups.

"Dammit," she said. Which is what Sarah and I say when we have the hiccups. There was more laughing, a bit more crying, lots of hiccups and not enough words to string together a coherent story about whatever was wrong. So I just sat next to her on the bed, put an arm around her and let her cry on my shoulder when she needed to, and felt her twitch with each jump in her diaphragm.

We came downstairs together. She normally wouldn't let me hug her in public anymore, not even in front of the family, but she was more... pliable... that day. Sarah and I had learned to walk down the stairs together, in step, with one of my arms around her, not stepping on each others' toes or bumping up against the bannister. Miranda needed some coaching and some guidance, but we managed.

"We're having spaghetti," Sarah announced.

"Miranda, meet Doug, Susie's girlfriend," I said, hoping I had parsed the genderswap thing correctly.

"Hey," said Miranda. "So does this mean..." she said to Susie.

"I'm a boy today. We traded," Susie explained patiently. Like the tall people in her household were hopelessly antique and needed to be told simple things five times.

"Cool," said Miranda. "So usually my brother Susie sits in that chair," she said to Doug. "But that's for girls, so you get it today."

She--Doug--beamed.

"What just happened?" Sarah murmured somewhere near my ear.

"Progress!" I said. It was one of those stock answers of which every marriage is full. Or so I imagine, only having been involved in one of them. Who knows. Maybe it was progress.

For myself, I've always kind of been comfortable being female, playing the hand I was dealt, with the advantages and disadvantages. Sarah's love was one advantage I couldn't imagine going through life without. I try to listen when I don't understand, and I know from the experience of friends that there are many ways to be queer, and some people don't fit in their skins. Sometimes it's biological, like Sarah, or Destiny, a ... I was going to say girl ... I knew once. A tale for another chapter, perhaps.

Sarah seemed to be okay with being female, at least most of the time, though her work on fertility, and the way we had become parents together of our remarkable brood of course tweaked her unrealized maleness. She didn't talk about it much, but whichever gender she was experiencing, she loved women, and, thank goodness, me in particular. I don't suppose it's possible to really understand why somebody loves you, so I just went with it, and tried not to mess it up.

Doug was polite, and I hope not overwhelmed by the estrogen in the room, and the realities of an all-female household. Except, of course, for Susie, who took her new role as man of the house seriously. It was cute, but in a way that had to be respected. A child's game, it turned out, but very real while it was going on.

It might seem quaint now, but we had a landline telephone. Which would invariably ring during dinner. Some people can just ignore a ringing telephone, but I am not one of them. So I answered.

It wasn't even a computer. "May I speak to the man of the house?"

Instead of the feminist screed I would normally indulge in, I put my hand over the mike and said, "Susie? He wants to speak to the man of the house."

Susie had abundant experience with us playing along with sales people on the telephone, so she grinned and said, "Sure." I gave her the phone.

In a soprano voice that could only belong to a seven year old girl, she said "Hello?" And then she giggled. "Aw, he hung up on me."

Doug was looking at Susie like he was her hero. She was his. They were theirs. Really, I try to do what transpeople ask, I mean, some of my best friends... Aaaand that sounded horrible. I have to say I was devoutly hoping this was a phase Susie would grow out of, for our convenience more than for anything in her own psyche. And for Doug, well, boys who want to be girls get the snot beat out of them, more often than not. Which is sad, but if he's really transgendered and knows it at age seven, it's a hard life he has cut out for him. I hope his family are supportive.

Chapter Twenty-Seven

Command and Control

Mo 2015

I kept badgering Sarah to keep up with the text messages from her family. I'm still not sure what actually happened.

So, OK, Lia was out of harm's way. Becca and Sarah put her on a train to Boston, to stay with one of Becca's exes and her... I was going to say menagerie, but that's cruel. Harem, maybe. I'm sure they're all decent people. Knowing Becca a little, I imagine they're geeky professor types who are remarkably creative and resilient in a pinch. Marines have no corner on the operative thing.

Miranda ran away the first chance she got, that same day that Lia left.

"What's up with Miranda?" I would ask Sarah.

And she would look at me like she had way too many things to think about and say, "Key West."

So I wheedled her numbers out of her mom and texted her myself.

"Lifeguarding off a tourboat," she replied. "Life is good."

"Glad you're safe," I texted.

"I should tell you about George," Miranda said.

Which, huh. I thought the whole thing came down when she discovered she was a lesbian. I mean, to each her own. And sometimes it took all day for her to reply, which makes sense if she's on the water.

And then there's Susie. At first it looked like she had just vanished, spirited away by the state. Becca's take, from talking to the guys who took her, was unfit parents, because they're gay and this is Virginia. But even here it takes some time to do the due process, and it was hardly an emergency.

Well, it was for Miranda, but Sarah managed to stabilize that. People need two parents to prevent exactly this: one kid gets hurt and the parents forget about the other one in the confusion. Lia felt awful, and it kinda made her nuts, which I totally understand. I was kinda nuts after I was unable to prevent... that... other thing.

And one thing led to another and now I'm arguably the only transperson ever to survive being in the Marines. Not the only one; there's a woman who was in Delta Force who's been in the news lately. Just one of the guys. Life is what happens while you're making other plans. Death also happens while you're making other plans. John Lennon was dead before he could make that quip.

Lia seemed to be doing well. She would text from her destination near Boston, where, um, I'm a little hazy on the people. Rachael I've heard of; Becca speaks wistfully of her as the third member of their, ahem, little commune thing, before they grew up and moved to the Confederacy and got all proper and monogamous and stuff. Rachael's ex-wife and her, um, friends, lived in a nice house in the Boston 'burbs and took in occasional homeless waifs like Lia.

And I do have to say that wow is the Commonwealth of Massachusetts different from the Commonwealth of Virginia, which decided the best parents I know were unfit because they were gay, and figured out how to terminate one of them who worked for a state university, with tenure no less, for the same reason. So she lands in a nest of academics up yondah who are openly gay and polyamorous. And not in fear for their jobs or their situation. It

NECESSARY LIES • 139

helps to actually own the house, of course. One wonders if the world can long endure such tension. It probably also helps that they're all white (well, except one who's Asian).

Anyway. I set my buddy Charlie the task of finding out what had become of Susie. And despite being a homeless vet, he knows people who know people, and he asked forgettable questions and got memorable answers, before they realized that the official silence had been breached.

All fingers pointed to the Committee to Re-elect the ~~President~~ uh, no, just the DA, which bore a remarkable resemblance to the old offensive line of the Clarke County Eagles Football Team. Which met under the watchful eyes of yours truly, in my real job as waitress.

James and John would come in pretty much every Tuesday for dinner, talk about strategy, not realizing that I might have a more than server-like interest in their conversation. 'Twas ever so, those in power not realizing the servants have ears.

And so a plan began to form. Sarah had been hard at work on the dress, doing forensic work, sequencing this and that. Putting together the case that somebody's father should have done, back when it all went down and he was the DA. Different district, different time. Good ol' boys watch each others' backs, and the little people get broken and smashed.

Charlie and I met up with Dweezil... his real name was something stupid like John Johnson. He'd been a journalist in the Corps, and we gave him an info-dump that could win him a Pulitzer if it were ever published. Corruption in law enforcement.

"There's a statute of limitations, of course," he pointed out.

"But the character of a political candidate is always open to discussion," I said, smiling.

"I like the way you think, ma'am." Always polite, that guy. And somehow he'd gotten the odd notion that my transition had placed me among the officer elite.

A plan began to form. We find a place, in public, where we could control all the alleys and streets leading out. With a squad of twenty homeless vets, most of whom had an axe to grind with the DA and the cops, that wouldn't be hard. We'd confront James and John with the evidence, with the fact that Dweezil had an article written and ready to go. We would demand Susie be released to us. It could work.

It would take nerves of steel, and those balls I had removed. Really, living without testosterone makes me much more level-headed in an emergency.

Cris needed to be in on it, of course. Because he's... she's... seriously badass. She nearly had the skills to take into the fight that night in high school. She has only gotten better, and the opposition has gone to seed, let me say it that way. Not that we'd want to assault the DA or anything, but... things could get... dynamic. Muscle and guile would be welcome.

Sarah, of course, who would be able to explain in terms even a lawyer could understand, just exactly what the forensic evidence showed. In terms a broken-down journalist could write up in a way that's totally convincing. I read it, I know. It's astonishing. It's rather a pity The Dweez might not get to publish it. If James goes along with it and we get Susie back.

We had a leak in our conspiracy, and I'm afraid it was me. Miranda and Lia were both texting me frequently, chatting about their lives, wondering what was up back at the ranch, and of course worrying, each in her own way, about Susie. Both of them not right in the head, though, and best kept out of the loop. And yet, I had to tell them something was being done.

So I think it turns out... I mean, this is the only way I can make sense of what happened. Miranda had another source of information; Vicky knew the family and she was still in the area. And so Miranda managed to figure out who Dweezil is, and Charlie, and Vicky came to talk to them, heart to heart, young girl to old tough Marine who hadn't actually talked to a girl (except me) in... years.

Vicky was easily as good at Jedi mind tricks as Charlie was. "Repeat after me... These are not the droids you're looking for."

Damn. Miranda should have married that girl when she had a chance. Not that she ever did, this being the Confederacy. Or ever would, if James had anything to say about it.

I don't think James was opposed in principle to gay people, but if he could use prosecuting them as a wedge issue, he didn't care who got hurt in the process. Something he learned on the football field.

Chapter
Twenty-Eight

One More Thing

Mo 2014

So, right. I almost forgot. This will be important later. There's this guy, Tom something... uh... DeSantis, his name is. He's a colleague of Lia's at GMU. So he's a bio professor of some kind. To hear her tell the tale, he thought he was sweet on her in grad school until he found out she was gay, and he and Sarah nearly came to blows over the favors of the fair maiden. I... sympathize, but she's very committed.

Sarah tells a similar tale without the flowers and unicorns. And more words like screams and pestilence.

Anyway, years later, Lia's department was hiring, and just to prove they're diverse, they appointed her to the search committee. Tom was job hunting, and his name came to the top of the short list. Lia recused herself, but he won anyway, and so there he was, installed in the next office over after all these years, setting up his own lab, teaching some of the same courses.

"It's kind of incestuous," Lia remarked once.

So sometime between Miranda's little incidents, let's call them, Lia decided a family day out would be just the thing. They invited me along; how nice. There's always one more thing to pick up at the office, so we pulled into the parking lot near Lia's place of business, and everybody went in with her for the last potty stop in civilization.

Tom was working Saturday, so one by one as people finished in the ladies' room, he helped us with the (entirely self-explanatory) water cooler. I thought he was a little too interested, but, like, whatever. Note to self: pay attention to something that doesn't feel right. He picked up the cups when we finished with them.

Anyway, we went off to the Blue Ridge, drove along the top for a while, hiked down the hill, and we admired brightly colored fungi, at least one of which burst open in a shower of spores. We also discovered that Susie's great going downhill but poops out going back up to the car, so I carried her up again.

To be sure, it's not a good thing to have to hike uphill when you're tired to the bone.

Anyway. It was fun. Lia had packed fried chicken for a picnic, and we found a ranger station that had a table outside. So the ants would take their sweet time coming to get the crumbs, long after we had gone. I think Susie was disappointed, but I remember Miranda being grateful for that, when I mentioned it.

While I was amusing the kiddies with tales of insects, their moms were looking into each others' eyes across the table. It was kinda romantic. Well, it looked like it.

"I'm sure you're probably tired of this by now," Lia said aloud, after a couple minutes of this. Not what I was expecting to hear.

"Not at all," Sarah said, putting her hand on top of Lia's, which was in the middle of the table. Again, note to self: pay attention to the details that are a little off. I can still read Lia like a book, and I could tell she was worried about the relationship. When Sarah gives something away, I should watch.

But no, Old Mo was helping Susie explain to her older sister how cool ants are. Miranda's not squeamish; I was more worried about fungus spores than either of them, for example. But she's a teenager, and Susie was teasing her about ants crawling up her legs, which gave Miranda the shakes. Susie thought this was hilarious.

I considered sharing the word of the moment with them: Formication, with an M in the middle, from Latin *formica*, ant, being the sensation of insects crawling on your skin. But there's no telling what use Susie might make of such a word, so I didn't mention it. I did tell Lia, later, after she remarked that I was smiling.

Anyway. A good time was had by all, subject to the usual family bickering, and the looming presence of Aunt Mo, who if nothing else knows how to run a wilderness adventure in which everybody gets out alive. We got everybody home safely, and Vicky showed up before I left the house. She and Miranda went upstairs together.

But thinking back, one imagines, putting clues together afterwards, that Tom was just as capable of sequencing DNA from a drinking glass as Sarah was, and his one-time (and continuing? If so he disguised it) romantic interest in Lia, he could easily have done a paternity test on the kiddies with the evidence we gave him that Saturday.

And if he cared enough to get some help, he could have figured out much of the rest of the family lore. But I was blissfully ignorant about all that, then. You'd think, being recently hired by a major research university, he'd have eyes on nothing but his research and getting tenure. That seems to be the way the life course goes, at least when Lia tells it. But no, he still had eyes for Lia, and more than idle curiosity about the paternity of her children.

I don't understand this part at all, but Lia knew that he knew. Maybe she just figured out that he could have assembled the evidence, and so, knowing Tom, she assumed that he had. Living with a secret tends to make one paranoid. I would know; trans people weren't allowed in the Marines when I was in, doing exactly that. Very quietly, watching to see who knew what when. Even though things are thin, financially, I much prefer this life to that one. Not to mention that it's safer (though still not entirely safe).

Chapter Twenty-Nine

The Why of Things

Mo 2014

After Vicky came to George Washington Hospital to tell her story to Sarah and Lia, I volunteered to take her home.

"So you're a friend of Miranda's mom," Vicky said, buckling in.

"We went to high school together."

"She's a little... off... somehow," said Vicky. "She's always been an attentive mom, once you allow for the absent-minded professor thing."

"Something kind of similar to Miranda's... accident... happened to us as kids. I think she's still having flashbacks," I said. "I volunteer with the war vets over at Walter Reed, and I know the symptoms."

"Aha," said Vicky. "Why would somebody do that?"

"Volunteer?" I asked, smiling, knowing that's not what she meant.

"No, beat up girls," said Vicky.

"Well, I was a boy then," I said, moving my knees closer together as I drove.

"Right. You're trans. I got that," said Vicky. The younger

generation astounds me sometimes. This is exactly how that conversation should go: it's a distraction, nothing more.

"Maybe we can find out," I suggested.

"Find out..." Vicky echoed. She'd be great in the Marine Corps, we do that there, too: repeat something if you don't understand.

"You know Sam," I said.

Vicky nodded.

"I have... ways... of getting people to talk to me," I said. "I'm kind of the Mother Confessor type, at least for guys who need to talk to somebody, get something off their chest."

"Mother Conf...," Vicky echoed. "Oh, I get it, like a Father Confessor."

"Except trans, yeah," I said. She's bright, this one. "I work in a restaurant; do you think you could get Sam to come in there?"

"I dunno. I'm not exactly on speaking terms with him, so I could ask him out or whatever," said Vicky. "Besides, he thinks I'm gay. So there's that against me, too."

"We might have to think of something treacherous, then," I said.

"Maybe in time we can come up with something," said Vicky. "So supposing..."

"Supposing..." I echoed, with a little smile.

"Supposing I talk him into going with me, do you need some

warning?"

"Text and see if I'm working that day, should be enough," I said. "I can almost always get somebody to cover if something juicy comes up. They know I'm good for covering them."

~

Mo, 2015

So months later, when things were getting pretty serious, Vicky texted. "You working today? I'm bringing him in."

"Him..." I replied.

"Sam," she said. "Sam, I, am."

"Sure," I said, and started buttonholing the other wait staff on my shift for a favor. We weren't busy that night.

The hostess seated Vicky and Sam in the far corner. I dropped by to chat, under cover of actually, you know, working there, and took the chair between where Sam was, back to the corner like a good soldier, and his only way out (bad soldier, getting boxed in). I removed my apron.

He glanced accusingly at Vicky.

"Don't blame her," I said. "I put her up to this. We just want to understand."

"There was a time I wanted to hurt you," Vicky admitted. Then she shrugged. Sam and I watched the way she moved. I could totally see how she wheedled information out of my homeless army, guys who hadn't actually talked to a cute girl in years. "Now? I just need to know why."

"You're gonna put me in jail if I tell you anything," said Sam. "Or try anyway."

"Nah," I said. "There are worse places than jail. I've been there. I'm back now. Some of the guys didn't make it."

He looked at me, in the eyes, for the first time.

"Wait," he said, "you're..."

"She's trans," said Vicky. "Ho hum. Deal with it."

I nodded, on cue.

Sam's mouth opened, and it closed again. "So..."

"Yup," I said. "To whatever you're about to ask."

"Can we get back to the why thing?" Vicky asked. "Other people's transitions are not your business."

"Well, unless...," said Sam.

"Unless..." Vicky parroted.

"Well, so. It never occurred to me that gay people were a real thing," said Sam. "I mean, sure, we talk about them in school, you read about them online, there are parades, people snicker and call names. Those folks are only out after midnight or something, right? That's past my bedtime. And then we'll grow up, graduate, stop picking on people (I hope... do we stop picking on people?), get married, raise kids, just like our Daddies did. Forget about school, and math, and the gay agenda or whatever."

"Is that related to fractions?" I asked. "Sorry," I said, looking at two confused teenagers. "Quoting Winnie the Pooh."

"And then bang! Miranda comes out, right in my lap almost. Well, conversationally. And she, well, both of you, walk right out of the whole gay mythology thing. It's like meeting a real, live Dinosaur or something."

"Who you calling a dinosaur?" Vicky demanded, moments before I said the same thing. We grinned at each other.

Sam looked up from his hands, at Vicky, and then at me. "Aaaand then of course I had to think about the five percent thing," said Sam.

"Ten percent," Vicky insisted.

"I suck at math," said Sam. "But if there are a hundred guys in my gym class, five of 'em are..."

"Gay," I said, "Just to put it right out loud."

"Right. And you wonder who's looking at me, and what that meant, and whether looking at him, in the shower, like, where he's soaping himself..." He glanced shyly at Vicky. "Sorry," he mumbled. "Did that mean I was... fuck no (sorry), but, but, but."

"Quite a rabbit hole," I said.

Vicky nodded. "It was kinda like that for me, too, except I knew I was," she said. "Aaand we're not talking about me. Sorry."

"I thought I was going crazy for a while. I mean, everybody was on edge, checking themselves at every moment. All those commonplace *That's so gay* things were suddenly... true, in some real way. Well, possibly true. What does truth even mean? When the grass is already on fire, playing with matches is no problem, right?"

"Oooh, a metaphor," Vicky teased.

"So you're pleading insanity, is that it?" I asked Sam.

"No," said Sam. "I'm sane. I'm straight." He glanced at Vicky. "I'm male." He glanced at me. "I know all these things. They have to be true. They have to."

"What is truth?" I asked, quietly.

He looked up at me suddenly. "Truth is making it all go away. Truth is putting the genie back in the bottle, without any wishes. Welding down the stopper forever."

"Poor genie," said Vicky.

He turned his head to look at her. She stared back at him, with a mixture of pity and fear in her eyes.

After a long silence, it seemed the adult present should do something. "You need a job? We're hiring busboys and dishwashers."

"I do, actually. You'd hire me after I told you all this?"

"Better to keep an eye on you," I said, and I smiled. Sweetly, I hoped, but sweet was far from my mind just then.

When the waiter came back, I asked for a job application for our friend. He nodded and brought one along with the check, which I paid.

"Did you learn anything?" I asked Vicky, when he had left.

"I... wow," she said. "I'm not even sure. That part about erasing us was... scary."

"The sad thing is, he might be queer himself. Not that he'd ever admit that."

"It took me long enough to admit it myself. I might still be wondering if Miranda hadn't..."

"Come out, right in your lap." I smiled. "He does have a way with words."

"Yeah," said Vicky. "Whoosh."

Chapter Thirty

Exile

Lia, 2015

It... got to be a bit too much, me living in a house with four polyamorous lesbians ("I'm bisexual," Andi would remind me whenever I said things like that.) Not that they weren't attractive, but my choices are not theirs, and both parties had some trouble realizing the other is for real.

Rachael was living in an apartment in town by herself, but I guess she felt responsible for me being there, what with being a friend of a friend. So she used that as an excuse to come over to dinner pretty often. And sometimes she stayed the night. Which, for those of you who are counting, meant five of them in two beds, plus me occupying the other one alone.

"Y'know," I said at breakfast the next morning.

"Never start a sentence with *Y'know*, it's always bad news," said Joy.

"I thought it was *Look*," said JJ. "From *The Way We Were*."

"What. Evar," said Andi, and then of course they all had to say it, imitating the undergraduates. We had a good laugh.

"You were saying..." Ravyn prompted.

"It might make sense for Rachael and me to trade places," I said. "She seems to come over here a lot." And immediately I regretted my choice of words.

"She said *come*," said Joy.

"Yes, she did," said Rachael. "And I do." She was grinning. "That's a really interesting idea. My lease runs through August, so if you need to stay til then, we wouldn't even have to do any fancy sublets or anything."

Somebody had to ask the homeowner, so I did it. "How do you feel about having your ex under your roof again?" I asked Ravyn.

"How do you feel about having your ex's fingers under your..." said Joy.

"Hush," said JJ.

"Yes'm," said Joy. They looked at each other for a minute or so, hardly blinking. "Normally I'd say it thrills me when the sub wants to be dominant," she said when the spell was broken. "In deference to our guest, I won't."

"You just did," Andi pointed out.

"Subjunctively," said Rachael.

"I'm good with it, if you are, Rachael," said Ravyn. "You seem to understand the dynamics around here pretty well. We are still officially married, for whatever that's worth."

"Might be useful, I suppose?" I said. "A couple with a few friends staying. They don't need to know about the benefits."

"Sometimes the truth is a lie," said Ravyn.

"Sometimes it is," I agreed.

In a week or so we commandeered a pickup and swapped Rachael's stuff for mine. I got to keep most of her furniture, since the house was furnished already. So it really was pretty much one small truckload in each direction.

I missed the sexy banter. I did not miss the unceasing sexual innuendo, which included me to the extent that I'm also a lesbian, but excluded me because I'm not that kind of a girl. The tension between inclusion and exclusion was hard to navigate, and there were times I got into trouble, at least verbally, since there are always people around willing to twist innocent words into a sexual advance. Among themselves, that's fine; they seem to be willing to put their lusts where their words are. With guests... Not so much.

Still, there's something heartwarming about seeing a bunch of queer women flouting society's expectations so completely and loving every minute of it. Everything is more complicated when there are kids. And where our very relationship is illegal, or at least extralegal. And where other truths also turn into lies.

Chapter Thirty-One

Living Alone

Lia, 2015

Living alone gave me more time to obsess about what was happening to my family. From time to time Ravyn would invite me over for dinner, and the company was good, and they jollied me out of my funks and depressions, by the simple expedient of serially propositioning me, each one of them. Like, right around the table. "Fuck!" I would say, about something in my life. "Okay, sure," would, invariably, come the answer, but from a different woman each time. It made me laugh. It did not make me horny. I think they were horny, always. All of them.

Did I mention that Tom managed to get me fired for being gay? The governor quietly deleted the equal employment executive order for state employees, and so since George Mason is a state institution, and there was this scandal about gay parents being unfit... While I was busy being crazy about Miranda and Susie and myself, they fired me. In the twenty-teens. I couldn't believe it either. Another thing to say *Fuck!* about, around the dinner table at Ravynscroft.

Sarah wasn't communicating, but Mo was, and she also seemed to be texting with Miranda. Who, come to think of it, didn't have a phone when I left. She must have decided she couldn't live without one. She's a teenager, after all. For another year and a half or so.

I did not like the sound of what Mo and Sarah were planning. With Cris, who was no less creepy than she had been when we finished high school. That stare into your eyes, letting you see all the pain in the universe in hers... The abyss stared back at that one, really deeply.

Where did we go wrong? Another unanswerable, imponderable

almost, that nonetheless I had to ponder answers for. It was so... fairytale perfect, those first few years. Then the struggle to conceive. I guess that's hard for a lot of couples. Not like for us, where Sarah was working flat out on her research, with us as subjects, and trying to be at least a little romantic at the same time. Because getting pregnant is supposed to be romantic. Even lesbians believe that lie.

It was not romantic. Well, mostly. There was that night at the hotel where we used to have trysts, when we were first... together. Long before they let us get married. But mostly there were lots of bright lights and cold metal tools, glassware and bleach and autoclaves. DNA sequencing when it was pricey, and since all this was under the table, budgetary backflips to get it funded somehow. Sarah's boss, Boris, was on board, even though it could arguably cost him his job and his reputation. But Sarah can be quite persuasive when she has her mind set on something.

What was it she used to say? Work hard, do your homework, cheat a little when you have to.

And we had two wonderful daughters. One of whom turned into a remarkably typical teenager.

"Were we ever that sullen?" Sarah would ask me in bed, talking about Miranda.

"Nope," I told her, and I did that thing of looking into her eyes to convince her I was telling the truth. Sometimes it worked, even with her.

Here's to you, Liz. Thanks for teaching me how to lie.

Where did I find Sarah, anyway? And how had she swept me off my feet, convincing me it was worth throwing caution to the winds to be hers, to do what she wanted, which was to prove those doctors wrong. I told her once in jest that I wanted to have her babies. When I found out what she was working on, I told her seriously that I wanted to have her babies. And that's exactly what we did.

That makes me sound like she used me.

Who knows. Maybe she did. It was so good, through so many years; does it matter?

Chapter Thirty-Two

Cilla

Lia, 1996

Like generations before me, I moved across country for grad school, to a new city, where nobody knew me, and I could rewrite my life any way I wanted to. The first couple years were okay, I guess; took a lot of classes, did a lot of homework, didn't notice the loneliness that much. Because I was learning the secrets of the universe. Reading the genetic code... I mean, all this information, passed down from... creation, really. When the world was much younger, certainly.

I used to wonder how we'd recognize non-human intelligence if we found it. You'd think finding an encyclopedia of life, that would do it... complete with instructions for copying itself.

Which I guess is why it doesn't violate the laws of thermodynamics... Once you have self-replication, you can really generate entropy, and getting more complicated is not a problem, if the complexity serves the survival of the critter involved.

The third year began, and I slid into a research group, having accomplished my exams. Learning to do wet work in the lab... Biology does seem to prefer aqueous solutions, at least at the molecular level.

And there comes a need to unwind. What with carefully sitting in the same position on the stool at my bench for hours, peering into a microscope, or feeding hundreds of pipettes. They could automate this, but of course it's our job in academia to show that it works, before it's worth making machines to do it quickly.

The guys were rubbing the knots out of each others' shoulders at the end of the day on Friday, so I joined them. "I'm pretty knotty," I said, and Tom nodded, rubbing my muscles with his thumbs.

"We're going out for beer," he said.

"Do they have stools? Because... no," I said.

Everybody laughed. "Booths," said Tom.

"Okay, then," I said. And to everybody's back I remarked, probably too quietly, that I'm not really dating, so.

I ended up curled into the back corner of a booth. They had food that was hot and greasy, and good beer, and we joked about biology and work and the faculty and post-docs and convinced ourselves we were feeling better about the world, the university, and ourselves. Ah, to be young again. Grad school is full of slights; you're in the big leagues now... your work should be really good. There's plenty of room for feeling inadequate.

Grad students are creatures of habit, and we ended up there every Friday for a long time. And every Friday, Little Miss Small Bladder had to either bully the guys out of the way or climb over them to get to the bathroom.

"You don't buy beer," Tom said once while I was more or less in his lap. And more or less still in my dress. "You just rent it."

We bumped heads laughing at his joke. I didn't quite pee on him, but it's dangerous, this humor thing.

And, um, so, Thanksgiving. People travel, apparently. I didn't really get my act together that year, but Cilla did, so she came to visit. Tiny apartment (but no roommate!), we lived in each other's back pockets for three days. The lab director had dinner for homeless waifs and grad students at his house. It was nice. I brought Cilla.

"Cilla, the guys. Guys, meet Cilla."

"So you know Lia then," Tom said. Captain Obvious, that one.

Cilla nodded.

And he'll comment on her stature in three, two, one...

"You're just her height," said Tom. I wonder if he could hear my eyes rolling.

Just like in the bar, we ended up squished together in the corner of the sectional in the living room, having to climb over people to get to the bathroom. Now, she didn't really have to accompany me; it's a private home after all. But being alone with all the guys maybe was daunting for her?

And the door was not fully closed before she grabbed me by the jaw and kissed me. Easily visible in the mirror to... Tom, who just happened to be the guy sitting in the right place.

"I'm not exactly out here," I breathed in Cilla's ear.

"You have never been in, in your whole life," she laughed.

"It's that obvious?" I asked.

She nodded. I tugged down on my dress as we rejoined the guys. Tom was watching me. Over dinner, Tom was watching Cilla.

After dinner, there was some kind of a parlor game where you get a word to make the rest of your team guess, and you can say anything not involving any of the synonyms listed on the card. It was actually kinda fun.

My word was "catalog" and so of course I thought of the course catalog with the red cover in the old days when they actually printed stuff for undergrads. We called it the Bucky Book. But then everything else in that town was Bucky's something or other.

"Bucky!" I said, intending to say "book" after. I only had two words to blurt out, and I failed.

"Gay bar!" said Cilla.

Which, I mean, of course. It's where we met. And stuff.

The Right Thing To Do here would be to smile, say, "no", and go on to another clue before the egg timer expired.

The What Lia Actually Did Thing was to blush bright red and look at her hands in her lap, suddenly aware of how very tenuous her... my... situation was. Pretending to be a Good Girl, living the life of a regular person in a lab full of straight men.

"Time's up," said Tom, in the ensuing silence.

"It certainly is," I said. "Cilla, I think it's time to go." Both as in, leave the party, and as in, go back to wherever you came from and don't out me any more.

We had no place to go just then but my tiny apartment, nowhere to sleep but my twin bed, which we tried to share without doing anything. Not what you'd call a success oriented experiment. And like lesbians since Sappho first articulated the experience, of course I fell in love with her. Dammit. Oxytocin for the ... I was gonna say win, but it was more of a loss.

I wonder if there's an antidote. Some kind of anti-love philtre. But it won't do to ask at the lab. And there's Barry Fucking Manilow singing "Don't fall in love" in my head. All. Day. Long.

And she packed up and went back to wherever she came from. And I cried. I hated myself for loving her. I loved myself for hating her. I managed to keep it together at work, most of the time, but thankfully being the only woman in the lab, nobody would bother me, weeping in the bathroom.

If any of the clueless men in the lab noticed my little faux pas, they were polite enough not to say anything. So, life went back to normal, with fewer smiles dispensed by Lia, for a while.

I wrote long letters to Cilla, which I shredded and burned. Some of the stuff that had been in fashion when I knew her came back, and I got them out of my closet and wore them again.

Fucking Tom asked me out. Um, no. I guess he liked the same outfits Cilla did? I tried the "I'm not really dating," line. He kinda bought it, I think? He was disappointed, and I was sorry for that, but. I couldn't say there's somebody else; he might ask who and I suck at lying. Maybe pining for an absent lover; that would have been true at least.

In another way, though, everything I do is a lie. I mean, who am I kidding, wanting to be a researcher. And if Cilla is right, I'm not even very good about being in the closet. With all the lies and half lies and alternate realities...

Chapter
Thirty-Three

Unrequited Oxytocin

Lia, 1996

So all that unrequited oxytocin reminded me that I kinda need somebody around. Somebody who actually understands and stuff. Not like the guys at the lab.

Thing about a city is you can lose yourself in another part of town and nobody will know you. I guess gay people have been doing that for generations. Anyway. Cilla was history. All those unsent love-letters were ashes. I didn't actually like her, and thankfully she went back to the flyover zone and I could ignore her.

Well, now and then a letter... remember those? With her return address. And the heart would turn over and beat backwards and my stomach would get all earpy and. And I'd read it, because how could I not torture myself with that? And she was all happy or weepy or missing me or not missing me, and whatever she said just made me feel worse. And I'd write a polite response, half full of whatever Great Thing I'd learned that week. And it would be months before there was an answer.

So, what the hell. Friday, instead of going home to mope in my little apartment I actually put on party duds, got on the train, walked the wrong way from the station for a while before realizing my mistake, and when I finally got there, took off my gloves and scarf, drowned the memory of Cilla in a full pint of beer. Usually I order the smaller sizes.

Halfway down the beer, I spun the barstool around and spent some time looking at the crowd. They were clearing space in the middle of the floor, so once it was clear where the front row seats would be, I snagged one. I guess folks are expected to come in pairs, so there was an empty place just next to me. And a second cup holder for the beer I bought from the cute waiter woman just before the lights went down.

Back in the flyover zone there wasn't really a critical mass of queer folks to do something like this place: a gay bar, complete with drag shows. I mean, sure, David was a queen, and sometimes we'd let him perform for us, but it wasn't a regular thing.

Miss Shirley was good. High glam, lip synching with no mistakes, making staying on top of her improbable shoes look easy, even when she was dancing. At least you don't need that much breath for lip-synching.

From time to time Miss Shirley would take the hand of someone in the crowd and dance with them for half a song. And then forget where they'd come from, parking them near any empty seat in the front row. So it was that the love of my life dropped almost literally into my lap.

"Where's my beer?" she asked, in the momentary silence between songs.

"Take mine," I said, having a second one as-yet untouched, ready for just such an emergency. "You're good," I said, referring to her dancing ability, but I'm pretty sure I was inaudible because of the music.

In a few minutes Miss Shirley was finished, and I wanted more of watching this woman dance, so I pulled her by the hand out of her seat and onto the dance floor. She was excited and happy and all of that got into my blood somehow. Note to grad student self: write a thesis on the communicability vectors for this kind of thing. If the microbes figure it out, we're all doomed. Bless their little pea-picking hearts. Nuclei. Whatever they have. Endosymbionts.

"Sarah," she said, taking my hand.

"Lia," I replied. "You're radiant."

"Just got tenure. I'm thrilled."

So, um, my alcohol addled mind couldn't do arithmetic any more that night but she surely had to be, what, six years older than I was, at least? But the sum wafted away on a haze of beer and smoke and loud music and we danced some more.

I still have no clear idea how she went from a random stranger who could dance to, um, your place or mine material. I don't think I've ever understood how I make that choice. It seemed so impossible, just that afternoon, and then it happened. I think Sarah was as surprised as I was.

Her place was nearby and didn't involve finding the subway station or walking far in the cold wind. The cold did blow a little sense into her head, though. She stopped at the door, turned around, key in hand, and asked, "What am I doing?"

I was not going home, alone, in that state, so I checked up and down the street for any audience there might be, and kissed her. I could feel a smile forming on her lips as I let her go.

"Oh right. That," she said, unlocking the door and letting us both in.

She flitted through the coming home chores: raising the thermostat, hanging up coats, feeding the cat. I think every woman I've known with a place of her own had a cat in it.

Come morning, I found a tall glass, filled it with water and drank it down. Perhaps in time it would fix most of the dehydration part of what ailed me. And I found the can opener where I'd watched Sarah abandon it, and fed the cat his (her?) breakfast. By then I thought maybe I had enough wits to rub together that I could face the coffeemaker.

Raw materials... There was a bag of beans in the freezer. Great. Dunno if I need a filter; must examine the apparatus. Which seemed to have lots of handles and lids and stuff. This was in the days before there was an industrial size espresso machine on every street corner, so I'd never actually seen one work. But hey, I'm a bench scientist, how hard can it be?

I must have been muttering aloud, because at some point I heard a smirk from the doorway, and there she was, a little rumpled, but grinning, and every bit as radiant as the night before. Even in the cold light of morning.

We looked at each other across the table. Sarah had found tiny espresso cups.

"High pressure steam," she said. "It's not something to mess with." So she showed me how the machine worked.

"It's okay," I said. "I wanted to make myself useful, but I do understand being checked out on the equipment."

She... smiled. And not about the espresso.

We smiled at each other for a long moment, while the coffee cooled.

"There's... a thing," she said.

"A thing," I echoed.

She had stopped smiling. She carefully upended the tiny saucer, dripping a little coffee back into her cup. "I don't know if it's ever happened to you. In fact, I hardly know anything about you. Except you can dance. That's a thing."

"So can you. It was fun."

"Yes," she said. "There was this librarian once. I, uh... took her home and kept her til she was past due. So to speak."

"Well, right," I said. "Cilla was a thing when we were undergrads. She came to visit over Thanksgiving. Like homing doves or something, she keeps coming back. Even though she's boring, just hanging out together... and stuff..."

"And stuff," said Sarah. The shy little grin was back. "Pigeons, anyway."

"Dammit, I fell in love with her all over again. I wasn't gonna do that." My hands were wrestling each other on the table, tying her nice cloth napkins in knots between their fingers. "So, yeah. Done with that. Not ready to begin again."

"I'm sorry you've been through it as well," said Sarah. "Let's just, I dunno, keep a few walls between us. For a while."

"Sounds wise. I don't know if I can do it, but it sounds wise. Put off all the weeping stuff until later."

"They say it always ends in tears. So let's just not end it," said Sarah. The full grin was back. The one from last night, that Miss Shirley put on her face. Because when the Drag Queen gets you to dance with her, you just have to smile, or run away.

"So tell me what you do," I said, half a second before she did.

"You first," I said, grinning. The wrestling of my hands had stopped. They were pretending to be proper sisters.

"Did I tell you last night they just gave me tenure? It seemed like such a long shot, but there it is. The labbies took me out to dinner, and I talked two of them into coming to the gayest bar in town. The rest of that tale you know."

"Nice of them to come along. I don't think any of my labbies know I'm gay," I said. "I mean, it's not exactly a big secret; I just don't date and don't talk about my personal life."

"And, let me guess, you live in a tiny apartment that might as well be a closet," said Sarah.

She makes me laugh. She still makes me laugh. It was pretty wonderful.

"Anyway," she said, "you're a molecular biology grad student, right?"

I nodded. She quizzed me about my coursework, and I told her what I dimly understood about our research. She seemed impressed that I mostly knew the big picture, as well as the single detail I had been assigned to pick at. So that will make a girl sit up a little straighter.

And then she started talking about what they do, which is studying fertility. How it actually works on a molecular level. And I followed for a while, before I stifled a yawn. We'd been up late the night before...

"'Scuse me," I said. "Can I make us more coffee?"

"You learn quickly and you saw me do it, I imagine you can," said Sarah. Annoyance number... well, I was gonna say one, but it was like six or so... word usage correction.

I smiled. She made one suggestion, and admitted it would work my way but there's a good chance of scalding yourself on the steam.

And the espresso came out nice and strong. "That'll put hair on your chest," said Sarah, tasting it.

"I, um, dunno what to say about that," I said. "I'm sure it's a metaphor and all, comma, but."

"Probably sexist. Dad was pretty unreconstructed, and I picked up a lot of his phrases. Sorry."

Somebody who apologizes. That's a plus. And if I'm making her rethink the way she talks, she must be feeling this, too.

"Better now?" she asked.

"Better..."

"Less sleepy, is what I meant," she said. The grin returned.

"Yes, thanks."

"I'm thinking there'll be lots of time to talk about what we do," she said.

"Cool," is the word that popped out of my mouth. You are not an undergraduate any more, Lia, and you should stop talking like one. Especially when a professor is romancing you in her kitchen on a Saturday morning.

Is romance even a verb, let alone transitive?

"So, um," said Sarah. Smile gone. The line between her eyes was back. Not the one in her lecture-mode face, the one in the talking about the librarian face.

"Um?" I prompted.

"This is probably getting ahead of ourselves, but," she started.

"But I'm just going to blurt all this out and we'll see what happens. I'm thinking of buying a house. I was even before the tenure decision, but now it looks like I'm staying, um, so, yeah."

"Um, so, yeah," I echoed, grinning at her. "Congratulations."

"I want you to come househunting with me. At least to get somebody else's perspective? Maybe? That's what I'm telling myself?"

"Aaaand, I'll do it," I said. "For another perspective. That's our story and we're sticking to it."

"Deal," she said. "Because we wouldn't want to rush..."

"Rush into anything hasty," I finished her sentence. "Before we..."

"Actually know each other. And I'm so glad you understand," she finished in a rush.

And I did understand, at least with my head. "There's this joke," I said, out loud, because... Well because it seemed like she should know more of what was in my head.

"What does a lesbian bring on her second date? That one?" she said, grinning.

"Yes! A U-Haul! It's funny because it's true."

"Well, it's hard to know how to conduct our lives, outside the legal and societal norms. Being gay is not for sissies," said Sarah. "Oh wait, maybe it is."

And the seriousness of the moment was broken. The negotiation over our future that was carefully not a negotiation over our future, was left unfinished.

Chapter Thirty-Four

Moving in Together

We went house hunting. Still pretending to ourselves, and each other, that I was just along for the ride, lending another pair of eyes to the assessment of various houses Sarah might be interested in buying, with her newly-minted tenured job and the promise of a steady income from academia. I mean, it seemed unimaginable from where I was, but obviously some people actually do make it.

The meanness of the agents at some of the open houses was breathtaking.

"I'm Sarah; this is my friend Lia," she would say, shaking his hand. Oddly the first dozen or so of these were all men. What ever happened to divorced women going into real estate?

"Just helping out," I would say in response to whatever he wanted to know about me. I did annoy several of them with the marble in my pocket, accidentally dropped to see if the floors were level. Some of them were obviously not; others I couldn't tell, what with the astigmatism correction in my glasses, until the marble tried to escape.

She eventually figured out what town we wanted, and found an agent of her own, who would then split the commission with whoever the seller had picked out. The guy drove us around, always with me in the back. I eventually found that if I sat behind him, I could exchange glances with Sarah in the front seat, and be out of his mirror's field of view.

We found one house on a chilly day when the sun came out suddenly as we toured the place. It seemed fundamentally sound;

NECESSARY LIES • 173

the floors were level, there were no obvious cracks or creaky noises or anything, and then... Oh, my, sunbeam in what might well be the master bedroom.

"So, what do you think?" the agent wanted to know, later that afternoon. There was some kind of wordless vocal music on the car stereo that... Well it didn't do much for me until two female voices intertwined in the upper register.

"There's that one," Sarah said, describing the house I just mentioned. "It seems... right, somehow."

"What's right about it? Maybe I can find a few more you'll like."

Sarah glanced over her shoulder at me in the back seat. I knew she'd seen me standing in the bedroom doorway looking at the sunshine. I checked to see that the agent couldn't see me, and, ahem, made an obscene gesture for Sarah's benefit. And then with a jaunty head motion wordlessly asked, "Are you in?"

She nodded almost imperceptibly.

"That one will do. What happens now?" she said.

The agent started talking about making offers, purchase and sale agreements, inspections, and I tuned out, or rather realized that, like the bridge in the music, we had just made some kind of commitment to each other. No words, just a nod of the head, acknowledging my gesture.

Not the kind of engagement one could write home about. Not that I had anybody back home I could write about it anyway. In time, they figured it out, but it was not a thing one talked about, either in the family, or in any other circle I frequented.

Well, except Cilla, and the other folks I had known as undergraduates. Somehow when I graduated, it seemed better to stuff that part of myself under the rug. Into the closet, I guess is how we say that. It would be coming out again very soon, when I moved with Sarah into this house she's buying.

One thing we would need is help with the heavy lifting. Neither of us is large or strong, and oh my do we have a lot of books. Sarah arranged to have a bed delivered, and the guys from the furniture store even set it up for us. But that left the books and shelves and Sarah's kitchen and, and, and...

"Hey, guys," I said that week at the group lunch. There's a big table in the office common room, not the actual lab, but we call it the lab.

So everybody turned to look at me. I don't mind if they do that when I'm talking about the experiments we do, but this was... different.

"So, um, I have some news," I said. You know how they talk about butterflies in your stomach? This was a pterodactyl, I think. Or maybe a hundred spiders, just hatched from a ball of worries.

"I'm, uh, moving in with somebody." My voice faded as it often does going into the second sentence, "And I want some help moving."

"Who's the lucky guy?" Fred, my professor, wanted to know.

How to respond. One, it's not a guy. Two, he shouldn't jump to the (correct in this case) conclusion that it involved my love life. Three, if he volunteered to help, which, I mean, he owns a truck, so... he would meet Sarah.

"Sarah," is the word that came out of my mouth.

Unreconstructed rednecks, all of them. Wait the requisite two clicks, three clicks, for people to begin to realize... Straight people. Can't live with them, can't seem to escape them. They're everywhere.

"Sarah Hartley. She's just been given tenure in the Fertility Research Center."

"One of those MD/PhD types then," said Fred. I could have survived just fine without that grin.

"And for those who are still figuring it out," I said, "I'm gay."

"Wow," said Tom. "I had no idea."

"Thank you," I said.

"For what?"

"Not noticing what I was trying not to show anybody."

"You're welcome? I guess?" Tom said. "And I also guess that explains... Oh wow. I am such a moron."

I watched him review his conduct throughout our relationship of, what, a year or two at that point. There was, as he said, much that seemed moronic from my point of view. Perhaps he would grow a bit, contemplating the situation in a new light.

Or, you know, maybe not.

Chapter
Thirty-Five

Job

Lia, 1997

So in due course, as it happens with most graduate students, my thesis came together, and I was duly certified as a world expert on one tiny piece of human knowledge, in my case the action of a particular enzyme. One cog in a very complicated machine. But the topic had been well chosen by my advisor, who, with Sarah's help, managed to hold me together long enough to learn some new things about it.

So I sent in the chapters, slightly rewritten to fit the style of various journals, and then sent out resumes and stuff to all the major research universities in the greater metro area. And just to be thorough, because Lia is nothing if she's not thorough, several other metro areas. The hope was, wherever I got a job, Sarah could also. I'm just starting out; she's a hot property.

Of course in those days it really did make a difference, at least as far as legal harassment, what state we ended up in. Boston? Married. All good. Atlanta? Never in a thousand years. DC, now that's an interesting case, because there are three different sets of laws that might apply.

With coaching from the labbies and from Sarah, I put together a very nice, polished, job talk, and went traveling. There were lots of interviews, and I learned to lie with a smile on my face. Of *course* I'd love to work here in the Deep South where you could fire me if you figured out my living situation. I love Southern Culture so much, what little I've seen of it. Eating biscuits and gravy is something I could actually enjoy, though of course some of the local variations were rather appalling.

But ultimately on the strength of letters from my advisor and

other committee members, I started getting offers, one of them
from a place just 20 miles from where Sarah was already working.
She wouldn't even have to move. How... convenient. We... wouldn't
even have to move.

Convenience is a bad word, in any language whose complexity
allows talking about life courses. The math people have this thing
called Incompleteness that Tom had tried explaining to me once. If
you can count, there are things about numbers that are neither true
nor false. Arguably Gödel was a madman, but he had a provable
idea. Though reality would be broken in a very charming way if it
had turned out that Gödel's statement was itself neither true nor
false.

It was getting dark by the time Sarah came home that day. I had
no idea; I'd been sitting there on the couch looking at nothing, eyes
filling with tears of gratitude every time I tried to reread the offer
letter.

"I'm home!" Sarah announced. She travels with more luggage
just for going to work than any woman I know. I heard her
depositing briefcase, backpack, shoulder bag on the bench in the
entry. For once, she remembered to put her keys in the bowl there; I
heard them clank.

"In here," I said, when the noise died down.

"It's dark," she said, "Just to state the obvious." She snapped on
the light.

At some point in my misspent youth I'd been part of a
discussion of *Romeo and Juliet* and what it meant to fall in love,
suddenly, at first sight. Now of course I'd been living with Sarah for
a year or more, but something in the change of my situation, that at
last perhaps I'd be worthy of being treated more or less as an equal,
plus herself standing in my living room under the light, scattering
from a thousand tiny fog droplets on her hair...

"Thou doth teach the torches to burn bright," I said. I managed to change *She* to *Thou,* but under the spur of the moment circumstances didn't get the verb changed to match.

"Dost," I corrected myself.

"Dust to dust, ashes to ashes," said Sarah, with a laugh. "What's up? What's that?" She waved a hand at the paper on official letterhead that was still in my hand.

My voice was unaccountably not working, so I handed it to her, she read it, and she held me while I cried on her shirt. Which was more or less what I would have been doing if it had been a rejection letter, though I would have felt much worse.

"This... plan we've made?" said Sarah. "It might actually work. How... amazingly bizarre."

"Yeah," I said. "Those guys in Virginia apparently liked what I had to say."

"And how you rearranged things to come to good solid conclusions, I'm thinking," said Sarah.

"Startup funds, my own lab, um gulp?" I said.

"Well, I was going to suggest going out for dinner, but..." She pulled at the tear stain on her shirt. "We can order in Chinese. Later."

And somehow I was laughing now as I cried on the other side of her shirt. It's such a relief, all that tension, all that pain, all those glimmers of false hope as it seemed then. And one dark foggy night, we plunged into full sun. The urge to hide behind... something, anything, was strong.

We... never ordered in Chinese. In fact I missed breakfast the next morning as well. But there wasn't anything pressing that

NECESSARY LIES · 179

needed doing at the lab, so Sarah let me sleep. About ten the phone rang.

"It's your wake-up call," Sarah said, laughing at me.

"It's... what... why..." I managed to paw most of the hair out of my eyes and was starting to work on the white noise between my ears.

"Congratulations again, Professor MacDonald," said Sarah, and she laughed at me again. "How does it feel?"

"Hung over," I managed to croak. "And, um."

"And, um," she agreed. "With you there."

Chapter
Thirty-Six

Going Home, I

Lia, 2015

I began to worry I would miss something important if I didn't go home soon. Sarah has this single-minded streak that won't take *no* for an answer. And I was afraid that Cris would be spoiling for a fight, and Mo was just kind of waiting for somebody to think up a mission for her to lead, like when he was back in the Corps.

And if whatever they had cooked up didn't work... Well, Susie would be even more gone, hidden deeper underground or whatever. I had fantasies of her being held by trolls. The literal ones, living under bridges, not the internet geekboy annoyances.

Like fucking Tom DeSantis. Who thought he was sweet on me in grad school. And whose name came to the top of the short list when we were hiring faculty, fifteen years on. I recused myself because I knew him, and damn if those fucking colleagues of mine didn't both hire him, and give him the office next to mine.

And fucking Tom still had fucking googly eyes when he looked at me. Despite having put on 40 pounds giving birth to Sarah's bastard children.

Wow. I'm in a mood today. Have I said "fucking" enough, do you think?

Tom would look at Miranda when she dropped by to wait for me after school sometimes. "She has your teeth, but Sarah's eyes," he said, more than once. And he's right, but I was sincerely hoping he wouldn't suspend his disbelief in parthenogenesis enough to seriously entertain that notion.

Yeah, I know. Hope all you want, Lia, it's all lies, mostly to yourself. I knew Tom, and I knew he'd survived grad school, which requires a certain gritty commitment to working all the way through things to find out how they work, come whatever may.

Working in a bio lab, DNA sequencing is all the rage, and if he wanted to sequence Miranda and do a paternity test, he was certainly capable of that. We're not MDs here, but like academics everywhere, there's a certain *How hard can it be?* attitude. And it's not that hard, but there's a whole lot of stuff to learn.

So there's this guy Sarah knew, and she had the unfortunate duty of being on the committee that investigated his academic misconduct. He was dismissed from GW for cause, which is unusual enough to make enemies for life. Tom looked him up. Of course he did. And between the two of them, they could figure it out.

When the Confederacy decided they had to fire me because I was educating their precious children to my immoral gay lifestyle choices, Tom was able to make ominous rumbling noises about unethical research. Which was not actually my research; just the way two creative lesbians had to use to make children of our own. I'm sure the Confederate Dead were rolling uneasily in their graves at the moral dreads.

Dammit, Tom. No, I won't fuck you. I'm a lesbian. Do whatever you need to do, just... not that.

So he did.

Revenge, they say, is a dish best served cold.

When the world came down around our ears, he was right there, moving and shaking.

Just because I'm paranoid doesn't mean the world isn't out to get me.

Chapter Thirty-Seven

Going Home, II

Miranda, 2015

Mo's texts were... I dunno. It was like she needed to talk to somebody who was far away, work through in her own mind what they were plotting. Which seemed... like cowboys and Indians or something. Too many spy novels. Heck. I'm eighteen, minus what, six months spent wandering purgatory; or does that count double somehow? Even I know this was unlikely to work.

So there was one slow day that Dez, the captain, let me bring George out to the mangroves along with just two tourists that day.

"I'm Miranda," I said, when they showed up at the dock.

"Bill." "Helen," they said.

"I'm George," said George. She laughed at the double-takes.

"Helen, meet Dez," I said to the wife. "She's the captain of our little boat."

"Hello!" Dez called from where she was pumping gasoline aboard.

George and I loaded the cooler into the boat, got out the kayaks and secured them to the poop deck or whatever you call it. The jumping-off place. I had learned that my George was hopeless about knots, so I did the tie-downs myself, just to be sure.

And we pushed off. Dez expertly guided the boat out of the

harbor and set a course northwest. She was giving the plan of the day, a spiel I'd heard a hundred times. A visit to a mangrove swamp, on a shoal a couple miles into the Gulf. And then a stop-off for snorkeling, where the water is about ten feet deep and there are lots of fish and critters on the bottom.

It was a pretty normal day. I got out the men's shaving supplies and told Bill to shave off his 'stache, demonstrating how a snorkeling mask works, without hair on the upper lip, and with. Helen laughed at him and took pictures of him doing it, and mugging for her camera afterwards. I pushed sunscreen on them. And for my George, who was still pretty pale.

I brought up the rear as always during the kayak excursion. Dez gives a pretty good biology lecture about mangroves, and my George was interested enough to keep up with the knot to be able to hear it. Three species, as you move away from the water, each less salt-tolerant, living in the silt captured in the roots of the last one. And there are lots of fish, and herons and stuff eating the fish. It's kinda fun, exploring an ecosystem that's so foreign.

Bill and Helen were thrilled with diving right in among the sea life, and he found a starfish that was moving along the bottom, hunting for clams or something. "Mask leaks when I smile," he said, when I asked if he was okay. This is the part of the day when I earn my keep, making sure the silly 'ristas don't swim out beyond where they can get back, or panic when they find the water is over their heads. My George is not that strong a swimmer, so I showed her how to float on her face, breathing through the snorkel, watching the fish go by underneath her. And then she went back to the boat to wait for us.

Anyway, back to harbor, bid Bill and Helen farewell, and get down to securing the boat with George and Dez. I turned my phone on again.

"Oh, my," I said, before I could shut my mouth.

"What's up?" Dez asked.

"My kid sister's been missing for a while. Something's happening."

"Okay, I need the whole story," said Dez. "It's been a while since I took you out for fish and chips. You two want a little supper?"

So there we were at some place with a name like Captain Jack's. They knew Dez, and they seemed perfectly okay with George and me sitting very close together.

And the whole sorry tale poured out of me, into Dez's sympathetic ear. I hoped it wasn't too much for George to hear, because, after all, we were sleeping together whether we wanted to actually *sleep together* or not.

"Can you send her a message?"

"Her..." I said. "Everybody in my life seems to be female."

"Susie, your sister."

"Maaaaaybe," I said, considering. "I'll try to wheedle her digits out of Mo."

"She should come here," said Dez. "Lots of people come here to get away from something. Present company included."

My mouth opened, and then it closed again. "What an interesting idea," I said.

"I've been thinking the same thing," said George, grinning. "Less practical, because two people in a twin bed almost works. Three..."

"We'll find a way," said Dez. "Did you say your mom was Lia

MacDonald?"

"Yeah," I said.

"I knew a woman by that name once. In college." Dez looked around and spoke in a lower voice. "She was kinda running the queer student alliance or whatever they called it."

"Huh. I thought she wasn't out til she met Mama."

"Well on a college campus far from home and everybody who knew you before or after, out is a little easier," said Dez. "Ask her if she remembers Destiny sometime. It's a silly name, but it's what my parents called me." She paused while the waiter refilled our tea. "You grow up, you decide it's easier to go along. I decided to be a woman, so I shortened my name to Dez."

"Not only is everybody in my life a woman, I think everybody is queer in some way or other," I said, smiling. "Life is a funny thing, isn't it?"

"Yup," George and Dez agreed.

"Seriously, though, if you can get Susie here, we'll make something work."

"Thanks, Dez," I said. "It's good to have options."

"We have to stick together," said Dez.

And George and I went home to our tiny apartment and peeled each other out of our bathing suits.

Chapter Thirty-Eight

So, How to Say This

Miranda, 2015

It was Tuesday. We both had Tuesdays off.

"I dunno how to say this," I said, sitting at the tiny table we shared. There were two chairs, but one of them lived between the table and the wall, until it came time to actually sit in them, and we'd pull the table out a few inches. Then one of us could sit in the corner and the other between the bed and the kitchen fixtures. The corner person had to walk over the bed and do a contortion to get into her seat, but it was possible. I suppose if somebody hurt herself, we might have to trade places for a while.

George sat down, swiveled to retrieve the fruit bowl, put it on the table between us, and then retrieved the coffee pot in the same way. "What's up?" she said.

"I kinda think I need to go home," I said. "At least for a while. Susie, my sister? They're gonna try something to spring her. I think."

"She's the one in foster care," said George.

"Right."

"But you'd come back, right?" said George. She held her hair in one hand off to one side of her head, so she could look at me.

I felt... I dunno, remorseful or something. Apparently she could read that on my face. Her lip wobbled and a tear escaped from one eye, ran down her nose and dripped into her bowl. Watching it go meant I didn't hafta look at her face.

"I've never broken up with anybody before," I said. "I've never even been with anybody before, unless you count Vicky, and the raciest thing we did was getting kicked out by the school librarian for not containing our screams of laughter when she kissed me in the stacks."

"There's probably a song about this," said George.

"Probly. Though they don't seem to write songs about not-quite-lesbians falling in... is it love, that we're in? I've never done that before either, and it's not anything like what I expected. Like toadstools when you were expecting shiitake or something. I'm not making sense."

"You're not making sense," George agreed. "And why am I so sad? I do hafta go home to Bill sometime, get him to give all my stuff back, at least. Why not now? I dunno."

"Make him call you George," I said.

"That would..." said George, stopping. "That would be a hoot, actually." She laughed, a little. "And tell me about the not-quite lesbians thing."

"Maybe it's part of the not recognizing love when it happened thing," I suggested. "It's supposed to be like falling off a surfboard and getting washed ashore, right?"

"Kinda," said George, laughing.

"Not like kissing a random stranger so that the guy behind her in line would leave us alone?"

"More like all the stuff we did after that," George suggested.

"Like each of us taking up more than half the space," I said, shrugging more or less by accident in the direction of the twin bed, which was nudging my leg at the table. Did I mention the apartment is really small? It's really a tight fit. "Which works if we fit together."

"Most of the time," said George, rubbing the latest bruise on her elbow. "I only get slammed up against the wall once a week or so now."

"It's like one of those martial arts, where you spend weeks learning how to fall safely," I said.

"True," said George. "And the... other stuff..."

"Is that all there is?" I said. "I mean, I dunno what I mean. Is that all there is? This is love?"

"I do love you," said George, looking me in the eyes.

"I love you too," I said. We'd been saying that for months. But then I had to add, "I think?"

"How romantic," laughed George. "But I think I know what you mean."

"If you think about it, it's very strange..." I said, intending to say more but somehow there weren't any more words.

"Strange things in my soup..." George sang, quoting a Sesame Street song or something.

"I mean," I said. "I dunno what I mean."

"You say that a lot," said George.

"I wonder if we'd even like each other if we weren't, like, um," I said, shrugging in the direction of the bed again.

"In this little space?" said George. "If we had to keep our hands off each other we'd need more room."

"Yeah," I said. "I'm not so sure..."

"Well, maybe when your family thing is sorted out you'll find somebody you are sure about," said George. "And now you mention it, I'm not so sure either. Bill was, well, fun for a while, but he got old. We got tired of each other. Not like this," she said, with a shrug that seemed larger than mine somehow, encompassing the whole tiny apartment, not just the bed.

We looked at each other for a long time, and there is this moment where you have to wonder what it was you saw in your partner in the first place. Boobs had a lot to do with that, I'm thinkin.

"So what happens now?" George asked.

"Um, I think we have to give notice on the apartment if we're moving out," I said. "Like in writing or whatever. I don't suppose you have a stamp."

"Nope. You?"

"Post office," I said. "Add to the note-to-self. And clean."

"How do we clean this place where we can't even turn around?" George asked. "Unless it's together. And the together thing is what got us into this in the first place."

"I think there's a management company in town someplace;

they prolly want the keys back," I said.

"Yeah."

"And Dez probably knows somebody who knows somebody who's driving to Miami sometime soon with an extra seat or two in the back. No way I'm hitching again." There were some... moments... on the way down here.

"I have bus fare home, when it comes to that," said George. "I'm gonna miss you."

"Yeah," I said. "I'm gonna miss you, too. My first real... whatever you are."

"My first girlfriend," said George.

"Yeahthat," I said. "Maybe if one person stands on the balcony holding an armload of stuff while the other scrubs..." If there's something practical to think about, maybe it won't be so sad.

"Could work," said George.

We cleaned like mad. In the end, we slithered together into the booth type shower, and when we were tired and sad and clean, into bed for one last...

One, Last. How very sad. Almost it was enough to change my mind. It's so much easier to stay. And for once, I didn't mind being so chummy she was almost inside my bikini with me.

~

If I was expecting to leave behind the lump in my throat, it didn't work. I thumbed out of Key West with a lesbian couple. We dropped George at the bus station. Changed rides in Orlando and

Atlanta and someplace in North Carolina. I remember lots of jokes about the Research Triangle, bumming rides with women who were clearly more into each other than me, but maybe wanted a taste of my imagination. And my Research Triangle, apparently.

Tysons Corner, Virginia. Backpack, myself, street corner. Home, kinda sorta. My thumbs seemed to know Vicky's digits.

"Hey," said Vicky, picking me up like a hitchhiker. Which is what I was.

"Hey," I said.

"Susie," Vicky said, before I could think of a way to say *sorry i ran away and stayed for a year and fell in love with a girl named George and got a life that didn't involve you.*

"Susie," I repeated. "Mo texts me sometimes, and I'm confused about what's going on."

"Something dire. The school district? I think? Child Protective Services? Somebody... declared your parents unfit and took her away to a foster home or something," she said. "Every time I hear that phrase I think of Stephen Foster and Way Down Upon the Suwannee River, Far Far from Home."

"I imagine that's how Sooz feels," I said. "And I was actually there, uh, a day or two ago."

"There?" I had forgotten that she didn't really follow the MacDonald-Hartley household free-association banter very well.

"Crossing the Suwannee River. It's in Florida or Georgia or somewhere."

"Ah," said Vicky.

"There are remarkably easy ways of getting away, if that's what's needed," I said.

"Maybe that's exactly it," said Vicky. "Just remember she's ten."

"Uh, yeah, that'd be more complicated than thumbing across the country at seventeen," I admitted. "Does Susie have a phone? Can you text her?"

"Of course," said Vicky, like I'd been out of commission since the Clinton Administration.

"Maybe we can like meet her in a park or something and... just kinda... never come home again," I suggested.

"She's watched pretty closely, she says," said Vicky. "Could work, but it's not going to be easy."

"What's Mo up to? My mom, Sarah, doesn't do the texting thing, and it feels like I hardly know her anymore," I said.

"She misses you. She's caught up in Mo's commando something something," said Vicky. "I dunno what."

"There's a restaurant she works at. Maybe we could just drop in and say hi," I suggested. "Stockyards or something, here in Tysons Corner."

"I could eat," said the Vicky that I had known Before. She smiled the way I remembered falling in love with.

Wow. Falling in love. It's... so different from what I thought it was then.

"Oh no," said Vicky, halfway through dinner. "Sam is the

busboy."

And sure enough. "It was good to be in a new town, where I didn't know anybody," I said. "But Mo is on tonight, at least. She's over on the other side."

Sam stopped at the table for a moment. "Hey, it's Miranda and Vicky. Sorry I was such a jerk." And he was gone before I had time to even think of a response. I mean, he probably tried to kill me with his truck, so that kind of apology doesn't really do. But at least he's realized he's a jerk, which is something.

We looked around for Mo when we cashed out, but she was nowhere to be seen. So we went outside, and on a whim turned right instead of left toward the Metro station.

And Oh. My. God. Everybody we knew was there, in the street.

Chapter Thirty-Nine

Lia Counterplots

Lia, 2015

Whatever was going down, I had to be there. Susie's my kid, too. I locked Rachael's door, pocketed the keys, took a cab to the train station, and was on my way. To what, I couldn't say.

And the tape replays again and again, that day, that awful day, when I was so worried about losing Miranda that I lost Susie instead. Kids have two parents, I keep telling myself, so that at least one of them will be available if they're needed.

Note to self, I dictated, in my imagination. *Ask Sarah why just two parents.* Because, wow, does that ever open things up, if kids can have other numbers of biological parents.

Six-thirty. Tick. Sarah stops by for a quick kiss and to tell me they're taking Miranda to George Washington, across the river.

World split. In the actual history, Mo drives me over the river and through what once must have been woods? Surely? To grandmother's house. To the GWU hospital.

In today's rewrite, I say, fine, take care of her, and go home to get Susie. And maybe then go to the District, arguably kidnapping my own kid and interstate flight to avoid the evil school district and child protective services.

It was a hot night in June. And sure, my brain was addled; who wouldn't be? Well, Sarah, apparently. Who is this creature I married, who can keep everything straight in her head, work on several different projects at once, and not get confused?

Well, she does slip up. Left the phone on. So I, being her lawfully wedded spouse, at least on this side of the river, called up the where's my phone app, and presto! Tysons Corner, not too far from... Yeah, not going there. Searching nearby... somebody's Stockyard Restaurant. Sounds just seedy enough for Cris and Mo. Parking? Score.

This time of the evening the traffic should be manageable. Oh. Don't really have a car. Or, hey, the Metro even. It's a straight shot. Never mind all that, Lia, just get yourself there.

And I found the place no problem. It was kind of built into what might once have been a stock yard, in an otherwise industrial zone, not too far from the mall, and the Metro station. This late in the afternoon, most people have gone home. So it's just... the players.

It's like found poetry, really. Mo has friends everywhere on the street. She's been visiting vets in the decaying VA hospitals, catching them when they fall through the cracks in the system, showing them how to use what they learned in the war to survive the peace.

Cris is... Cris. She... he... whatever Cris is nowadays, left society behind, blotted out the signature on the social contract, and went her own way. Not so very unlike Mo's minions, but by a different route. I don't know that it started that night, that horrible night, when football team versus Misfit Toys went down, and we ended up broken and they went on to roll over the Rebs and everybody all the way to State.

Cris was standing two paces behind Sarah. Who looked scared, but with a brave face on things. She's not a tall person, and she was looking up at... Oh, God, it was James. James Fucking Crockett. Jimminy Crockett, we called him sometimes, when he tormented us in high school.

"Look," Sarah was saying.

And I wanted to quote *The Way We Were* at her: Never start a sentence with "Look," it's always bad news. But for once I stayed out of it, watched it unfold.

"You're the District Attorney now, not the kid who beat up on some girls with your buddies."

"I always knew you were a girlyman," James said to Mo.

That, right there, made my blood boil. Which oddly kind of cleared away all the other voices in my head. Anger as a tool. I should remember to use that. It also made me want to turn and run, but this wasn't about me.

Mo smiled. She'd been called worse things, I'm sure.

"But you do kind of want something," said Cris. "And that gives us some leverage. You'd like to be re-elected."

He tilted his head in acknowledgement.

"So, I'm no politician," said Sarah, "But I'm guessing it wouldn't look so good if certain things came out of your history."

"No evidence, no problem," said James, and he smiled.

Cris handed Sarah a nylon bag, one of the reusable ones you can get at upscale outfitters. "Well, not exactly," said Sarah. She pulled a few inches of purple fabric out of the bag. It was the crinkly stuff you can get at Tibetan clothing stores. And I recognized it immediately.

"What do you have?" asked James.

"Oh, nothing much. I think it was a dress once," said Sarah. She pulled a little more fabric out of the bag. "Kind of attractive, after all these years, though I imagine it was risque then. It seems to kind of tie on, wrap around... the least breeze would draw people's eyes."

She held it up. She had carefully tied the waist band to hold it together, more or less. The breeze did indeed make me wonder how anybody--how I in particular--managed to wear it.

"But it seems to be torn. How sad," said Sarah. "Not that it would fit, now days, anyway."

"How is Lia anyway?" asked James.

Cris had noticed me, and shot me a look to keep me quiet and out of sight.

"And stained, James. The dress has stains on it," said Sarah. "Modern technology is wonderful. Stains we could take samples from."

"And you'll need something to compare to," said James, remembering his legal training.

"Remember that waitress you failed to tip? That night last month when you and the rest of the Offending Line got together?" said Mo. "That was me. And I took the liberty of snitching your water glass. And the others. Marked them, I did. Combat medic training, make sure we know what body parts belong to whom so we can stitch them together again."

"Statute of limitations," said James.

"Rape," said Mo. "It's an ugly word. There's no statute of limitations for rape."

"The chain of evidence is pretty thin," said James.

"True. But we're talking the court of public opinion here," said Cris.

"And I could call for help..." James suggested.

"I bricked your phone," said Cris, chuckling.

"And who's going to believe a bunch of drifters and misfits?" James asked.

"That's not a problem," said Mo. She whistled, and a homeless man appeared at each of the alleyways or streets leaving the square, such as it was. "Hey, Dweezil," she called.

He waved.

"Dweezil used to write for Stars and Stripes when he was in the service. Mostly motivational stuff, but also some investigative journalism. Knows how to put things together so they stay. And he kind of resents being forced out of his residence by a certain overzealous prosecutor. He's got all the info, and a story ready to go."

I looked around the alleyway, with one or two of Mo's Vet friends standing, deceptively at rest, in each possible exit, and Mo herself with Cris standing behind Sarah blocking the way we all came in. James was nervous; he kept looking around. The silence was deep for a city; it was easy to hear what people said.

"There's nobody here to call signals for you," Cris mocked.

It tasted salty, like violence does before it starts. Or was that after. Maybe I picked up some of the gravel in my mouth. Do they use road salt in Virginia? I don't even remember. I know we get ice storms.

The sweep of events was tightening. Whatever it was would

happen soon. And in the Beyond, we would have the luxury of hindsight, the leisure to regret what we were about to do. But the agony of the last few moments of Before was exquisite. You could live your whole life and never see such a moment. Perhaps that would be preferable. Certainly avoiding the need to force such a nexus would be a wonderful thing.

As always, Sarah thought she had everything nailed down, that she could control the spin, ride the tornado.

But hey. I'm gay. People hate me. I know that; I don't understand it, but I know it. The universe hates me, I think. And they have my baby. The pointed end of whatever's coming down will hit me. Every time. I believe this.

I was not in on the plot; Sarah thinks I'm in Boston, unaware that my wife and my friends are plotting something. How could I be unaware? Susie is... over here someplace. Miranda at least is safe, far away in Sunny Florida. She's also tasted the salt of the Virginia gutter. I am so sorry, kiddo. I thought I had done enough for all of us.

And in that moment when the universe was balanced on a breath of air, I knew why it was I had called Tom DeSantis, of all people, to come witness this. He walked into the square. I had to make myself known. I'm sure Mo and some of her Marines had noticed me; they learned to notice everything to keep themselves alive. Sarah was surprised, and James flinched. I can't imagine where I found the courage to do that, to walk out of the shadows.

"You stay out of this, Lia," Sarah was saying.

"What's in it for him? He gives you everything you want and you... no longer have an incentive not to blow the whistle on him. I have a suggestion."

"We're listening," said Cris.

"We give you the family secret," I said to James. "You give us Susie, and we settle into a Cold War kind of detente of mutual assured destruction."

The silence got deeper.

"I'm interested," said James.

"I'm not," said Sarah.

"I'm tired of fighting," I said to nobody in particular. "This ends here, tonight. Tomorrow we all start acting like responsible adults again. Blackmail used to work, I guess. But it's unstable, from a game theory point of view. This way we both have everything to lose."

"I don't see how..." Sarah said.

"Tom?" I said, ignoring her. She was several years older, had tenure before I finished grad school. We had always done things her way. Conceived the girls in a way she had invented. Found a job for me, near her research institute.

Tom cleared his throat. "It seems I'm holding the bag here," he said.

"Briefly," I said. He does like to go on about things he's found out.

"Turns out," he said, "and I can fill in the details later, that they're not the only people with DNA testing." He waved at the package in Sarah's hand. "Sarah is... the biological father of both girls. Through some kind of reproductive research thing that's unethical in every way I can think of, and possibly illegal."

"It's true," I said. "And now you know. The truth shall make you free. Whether it makes us free is up to you. With a little incentive from that other genetic testing Sarah mentioned."

James licked his lips. On the football field he had been a lineman and not in charge of making decisions, but years in a courtroom had taught him how to think on his feet.

He nodded.

"Louder, James," said Cris.

"Deal. I'll call..."

"Bricked your phone," Cris repeated.

"I'll give Tom here the number, shall I?"

Nods.

Tom's thumbs were clumsy and it took him a couple tries.

"Joe? It's James. Remember Susie MacDonald-Hartley? We're returning her to custody of her parents. Tonight, Joe. Make it happen. Bring her to... the Stockyard Restaurant. And Joe? No cops."

Chapter
Forty

For a Black Op...

Mo, 2015

For a Black Operation, this one seemed to be really leaky. It's true that, while I'm good operationally when I'm not involved emotionally, Lia and her family are my friends, dammit, and I couldn't keep them in the dark.

So we had this wonderful plan all worked out. Me and the guys would seal off the exits, we'd surround James, and Sarah could negotiate from a position of strength.

I supplied the blackmail in the person of my buddy Dweezil, who's a journalist, free-lance, homeless vet, clean now, but on the pointy end of anti-homeless and anti-drug efforts on the part of the local cops, pushed, no doubt, by Mister DA James Crockett himself. No love lost there.

Cris supplied the devious mind that fit it all together. This girl... excuse me, this person... is totally amazing when the chips are down and I want her, him, whatever, on my side. It would help if I stopped pissing them off using the wrong pronouns.

Lia, because she's Lia, kept the dress. Sarah knew that, got her to retrieve it from the house, and then sent her into exile to be out of the way. Flaky people, people who are carefully constructed functioning personas on top of a volcano of unresolved issues... Yeah, not good in a fight. I hoped it wouldn't come to fighting, but if it did, we would kick ass and take names. Some of us would be better at melting into the underground than others. If it came to that.

All set up. I herded him into the trap, taking off my apron after serving his dinner. I think until that moment he hadn't figured out that I was little Maurice, whom he had picked on and beat up when I was a boy. I pass pretty well, I guess, but having no recognition when I was undercover was gratifying.

Cris had some malware on her phone, and he activated it as the low whistle signaled the troops to seal the place off. There was an electronic clang from James' pocket. Cris had a smirk on her face when he put his phone away.

Sarah presented her terms. She was just getting down to business when I noticed that Lia was in the shadows, within easy earshot. Great. I increased my level of situational awareness, trying to anticipate anything and be ready for it.

James wasn't going for it. Straight-up blackmail wasn't interesting to him. The way his eyes were shifting, he was calculating his odds of getting out of the alley alive (pretty good), being able to defuse whatever adverse publicity might arise (hey, they're just queers...), and getting re-elected. This is the South, the money was in his column, how hard could it be?

Lia cleared her throat and stepped forward. Now, in a negotiation, you keep your vulnerabilities as far off the table as you can. Lia's solution was something none of us would have thought of. Her colleague from George Mason, who'd helped getting her fired there when shit got real, yo, Tom somebody... She brought him along. Let's you and him fight kind of a scenario, I was thinking, watching our plans unravel. I couldn't imagine...

She put the family secrets on the table. Sarah was the father of the girls, who, speaking of, Miranda and Vicky strolled out of the restaurant into the side street just then. Dammit. Area security used to be my specialty, when setting up ambushes.

Lia, as I was saying, went for mutual assured destruction. That way if James thought we would divulge his secrets, he could talk about ours. Not in his official capacity, since none of the events happened in his jurisdiction, and if they did, Susie was ten already and that's probably about how long the statute of limitations would be for most things. But he could still get Sarah in a heap of trouble. And we could get him in a heap of trouble. And Tom was right there with genetic evidence of his own, proving Sarah's paternity.

James nodded.

"Louder, James," said Cris.

"It's a deal," said James. "I'll just call..."

"Bricked your phone," said Cris.

"I'll give the digits to Tom here, shall I?" James suggested.

So Tom dialed, while Cris checked the phone number. Wouldn't do to trust James. She nodded, Tom pressed the connect button, and tossed the phone to James.

"Joe? It's James," we all heard him say. "You remember Susie-- Susan--MacDonald-Hartley? We're releasing her to her parents' custody. They're not unfit parents at all. It's a big misunderstanding. Tonight, Joe. Bring her to the Stockyard restaurant. Oh, and Joe? No cops. Just you and the girl."

Cris' thumb was twitching on her phone, just in case, but James disconnected and tossed the phone back to its owner. Tom turned it off and pocketed it.

"We wait," I said.

Ex-Marines are good at waiting, patiently always at the ready, knowing this moment, now, when nothing's happening, is probably better than whatever might happen next.

"What's going on?" Miranda demanded. She just kind of

wandered into the ops zone with Vicky.

"Haven't seen you in a while," said Sarah. "Big family reunion, in the seedy part of town where we told you never to come on your own." There were hugs for Miranda from her Moms.

James chuckled humorlessly. I still had my professional eye on him. So did my squad of homeless vets.

The car arrived, the doors unlocked, and Susie bounced out, running for Sarah's arms. And then she saw Lia, so she pulled away, and ran to her other mother's arms.

We made an opening in the crowd for James to walk through, and he thought better of trying for the last word, got into Joe's car, and they drove off together.

I whistled the troops to relax. Dweezil wanted to know if he'd get to publish the juicy story he'd written. "Not right now," I said. "We'll keep it in reserve, in case the enemy turns hostile again."

"Yeah, I never really got the hang of peacetime," he said. "Thanks for letting me play."

"We'll be in touch," I said. "Semper fi."

"Semper fi," he said, and they were gone. It's easy to forget about the homeless warrior class living in our city, but they're always nearby.

"Where to?" I asked Sarah.

She looked at Lia, who looked back at her.

We all gave them a moment. Some things can't be rushed, and this was clearly one of those things.

"If people want food, there's a restaurant really nearby where I can probably even swing some discounts," I suggested. If they hadn't fired me already for walking out in the middle of a shift. If they had, well, there are other places that need servers, and it might not be wise to hang out so near the scene of the ... I was gonna say crime, but it wasn't. Evolution. A good Marine Corps word.

Chapter Forty-One

Shakes

Miranda, 2015

So, um, it was... awkward.

I dunno what Sarah had in mind for me when I got out of rehab, but I guess thumbing off to Florida wasn't it. She was busy trying to figure out what to do about Susie, though, so I just did what I needed to do, which was to be as far away as I could go, at least in the general direction I started out.

She had shipped Lia off to friends in Boston. Her tales of the lesbian commune make me want to see this for myself.

Sarah herself bought a house in the Maryland burbs, not all that far from the GW hospital where she worked. When she wasn't plotting various things with Mo and Cris.

Who, it developed, were living together somewhere in the low rent district of Tysons Corner. Made sense, financially; it was on the Metro so Mo could get to Walter Reed to do her vet thing, visiting with the guys who almost didn't make it. Recruiting an underground army, just in case she had to deal with... folks like our District Attorney, apparently, who essentially was holding Susie for ransom or something. All official and legal and with the right number of signatures in red ink, I'm sure. It always is. What they don't tell you is that the system is stacked against the likes of us, and it can be kinda snaky for insiders who want it to do something in particular.

Mo treated us to dinner on her employee card. Apparently it was a slow night otherwise, so since she had gotten other servers to cover, the manager was happy.

Susie babbled on for a while about her new school and Mr. and Mrs. Culpeper that she was living with. She was kind of amazed that there was an actual man, living in the house. I mean, the neighbors were all straight, more or less, so it's not all *that* weird. But I can see how, growing up in a lesbian household as we did, where most of the family friends were also lesbians, you might get the impression it was the norm. You know, by the numbers, even.

"One big happy family," I said, just to fill the silence.

At least Sarah and Lia were no longer staring daggers at each other. They were both looking at me.

"Yeah," said Sarah.

"I'm glad everyone is safe," said Lia.

"For how long, I wonder," Sarah mused, mostly to herself.

"James is managed, I think," said Mo. "Thanks, in no small part, to Lia's gambit."

"For how long, I wonder," Sarah repeated.

"You should read the article Dweezil wrote," said Mo. "Trust me, he does not want that on the internet."

"And when he wins the election?" Lia asked.

"Well, maybe we won't be in his district to see that," said Sarah.

"It does sound wise to get out of town," said Cris.

"And I didn't get my job back," said Lia. "I'm still gay, and

Virginia is still not for lovers, despite the bumper stickers."

"Maybe we can move to Boston," Sarah suggested. "Or just kinda drop out and tour in a VW bus."

"Are there any around that still run?" Mo asked. "If you took a couple of my guys along in a second vehicle to be your mechanics, maybe..."

"D'you guys really want to be that together?" I asked, wishing as soon as I said it that I hadn't. "I mean, there was this girl in Florida; my apartment wasn't all that much bigger than a VW bus. Well, it was, but you know what I mean. And, um, the chummy thing got kinda old kinda fast. Being lesbians we stuck it out way longer than we should have."

There was that thing where both moms were looking at me again.

"Lia?" said Sarah, looking at me and not her.

"Sarah?" said Lia, also looking at me and not her partner.

"How did two idiots like us manage to spawn such a wise kid?" said Sarah.

"I dunno," said Lia. "I mean, I remember the process, but, that's got not much at all to do with the woman she turned out to be. I guess we should be proud."

"I guess we should," said Sarah. "And we should be proud of our other daughter, who held on through whatever the foster care system put her through, while we figured out how to get her out."

"Vic and I were plotting to take her with us, thumbing out of state," I said.

"Really? That'd be fun!" said Susie.

"But the adults came to a nice adult solution first," I said. "Not that it wouldn't have been fun. My boat captain in Florida said she'd help figure something out if we brought you there."

"Florida sounds like fun," said Susie. "But I wanna be with my moms for a while, I think."

Lia was smiling sadly. "You make me proud, both of you."

"Oh, hey," I said to Lia. "Speaking of Dez, she wanted me to ask the next time I saw you, if you remembered Destiny."

"Do I ever," said Lia.

"She went to the end of the road like I did, bought a boat, and makes a good living off the tourists," I said. "She also said she decided to be a woman, whatever that means."

Mo and Cris started paying closer attention to what was otherwise family business.

"Well, I'm glad things went well for her. Him," said Lia. "Destiny was another one of my little projects in the queer student alliance when I was an undergrad," she said, mostly to Sarah. "I don't know if I've ever met another actual intersex person, who wasn't altered either surgically or by hormones without their consent. So she had the choice, at some point after I knew her, what to do with herself."

She chuckled. "And one of the Boston gang is laughing at me in my head, saying 'She said *knew*!' Which would be right."

And then she got all flustered, talking about her dating life in front of her daughters. Not to mention her wife, who was not all that thrilled with her just now anyway.

Chapter Forty-Two

Craving Affection

Miranda, 2015

OK, so Sarah had sold the house in Virginia. They weren't all that excited about actually living there again, after everything that came down on us there, so yeah, I kinda get it. It was sad, though, the way it was just gone.

Sarah invited Mo and Cris to move in to her house in the Maryland suburbs. It was a little chummy having all of us there. I'd been in Florida, of course, and Lia had been in Boston or someplace. But they put us up for a few days. There was lots of attention for Susie, who after all had just been sprung from state custody in Virginia. Sarah set up a room for her at the house.

"Wow, just like in Virginia, all to myself," was Susie's comment. "I had to share with two of the Culpepers' kids. They had bunk beds, which is neat. But they didn't really want me in their room."

Knowing a thing or two about sharing a too-small space myself, I could sympathize.

Eventually I managed to find Lia and Sarah both together, not fighting, and could help keep the not-fighting thing going by letting them focus their concern on me. I think Mo and Cris had taken Susie out for ice cream or to the zoo or something.

"So, um," I said.

And there was that feeling from my teen years of all the maternal attention being focused on me. But it was important, so I didn't wilt.

"Anyway," I said. "So I went to Key West, as I told you, and ended up kinda sorta accidentally living with a girl I called George, in a really small apartment. I mean, it was bigger than my room in Virginia, but also had a kitchenette and a bathroom and stuff."

"Mmmhmm," said Lia. "Kinda sorta accidentally..." She looked at Sarah.

Sarah looked back at Lia. "I was hoping the next generation wouldn't do that," she said.

"Accidentally forming lifelong relationships?" Lia said.

Sarah nodded. "Go on," she said, to me.

"Anyway," I said again. "Being in love, if that's what it was... it's way different than I expected. It's sorta supposed to be this huge tidal wave thing that sweeps you away. Not just, you know, kinda, hey, you need a place to stay and if we squeeze tight you'd fit in mine. I've heard your stories about meeting and it seems so romantic."

"Swept away by a tidal wave," said Lia. "Pretty much." She was looking out the window.

"Not so much," said Sarah. "I remember her saying, that first night, after finding out what I was working on, that she wanted to have my babies. And I looked at her again with that in mind, and like, sure, why not?"

Lia sniffled.

Sarah pushed the tissues across the table in her direction.

"I'm trying to put something together," I said. "I did some

reading..."

Big grins from my academic forebears.

"Shut up," I said, even though they hadn't said anything. "That genetic thing, CAIS you told me about," I said.

"Yeah..." said Sarah. "Complete Androgen Insensitivity Syndrome."

"Maybe it suppresses desire?" I suggested.

"Maybe so," said Sarah. "Sexual desire in humans is at least partly mediated by testosterone, even in women. So, yeah, being insensitive can make it hard to get excited. And I can't believe I'm talking to my daughter about this." She covered most of her face with one hand. But then she peeked out between her fingers. Susie does that sometimes, so I laughed.

"And it's inherited, as you told me. So if..." I turned toward Lia. "If the trait also runs on your side of the family..."

"I did try to get Sarah to think about that once," said Lia. There was an exchange of Highly Significant Glances between the moms. "I have a lot of maiden aunts, and not that many uncles."

"I sat down with the family tree when I started thinking about this stuff," I said. "Yes, sometimes Miranda does her homework. Jeez." The proud mama smiles were stifled.

"So what happens if, lemme see if I can get this right..." I said, turning back to Sarah, who after all studies this kind of thing professionally, and has the condition herself. "You're an XY female. The CAIS mutation gene or whatever is on the X chromosome. I have your X chromosome, so I have one mutated copy. From you. Right?"

"Right," said Sarah.

"And I have another X chromosome from you," I said to Lia. "Randomly chosen, I imagine, though you might have done some black magic..."

"Nope, random," said Sarah.

"Cool. Anyway, if my other mother is a carrier, she would have one good X chromosome and one with the mutation. And I'd have a 50/50 chance of getting either one."

"Right again," said Sarah. "It's unlikely she's a carrier, though. Only a few percent of women are..."

"Yeah yeah. Don't confuse me with the math," I interrupted. "The point (and I do have one, for once) is this: What happens if I have two defective X chromosomes?"

"I... don't actually know," said Sarah. "And neither does anybody else. You are probably the first person for whom that's been possible. Since I'm the first CAIS XY female who's known to have... fathered a child." She shuddered visibly at the word *father*. "Well, as far as I know. We didn't publish this research, so somebody else might have done the same thing and we wouldn't be aware of it. But yeah, you might be unique."

"And Susie..." I said.

"50/50 chance, if Lia's a carrier," said Sarah. "So it's rather unlikely you'd both be CAIS XX women."

"My point (and I do have one) is to ask this: What are the effects on me if I am such a person? Would the fact I wasn't swept off my feet when George fell into my lap explain that? And I'm tangled up in my syntax again. I blame head injuries or something. You get my question, though."

"Yeah, I understand. And it could be. Unlike me, you have essentially normal female anatomy, hormone levels, etc. etc. etc.," said Sarah.

"All those clinic visits when I was a kid," I said.

"Yeah. I certainly hated them myself, so I'm sorry we put you through that, too. But we had to be sure you're normal," said Sarah.

"Can you sequence Miranda's DNA?" Lia asked Sarah.

"Yeah, we can. It's not even expensive any more."

"And why do I think Tom DeSantis has probably already done it?" Lia asked nobody in particular.

"Because he's nosy and way too smart for his own good," said Sarah. "Oh, sorry, that was a rhetorical question."

The moms were smiling at each other for once. Score one for Miranda.

"To answer your question, I imagine that, like me, you'd have a harder time getting excited about, you know..." said Sarah.

"Sex," I said. Somebody had to. "Which maybe explains why the whole coming out thing was such a surprise to me, since I'm mostly lacking the basic instinct to mate."

"Not totally lacking," said Sarah. "I certainly crave affection," she added quietly, pointedly not looking at Lia.

"That's a good way to say it," I said. "And, um, you can go a long way on somebody else's sex drive," I added. When I looked up from the hands that were wrestling in my lap, I met Sarah's eyes. There were tears in them.

"Lia?" Sarah said, still looking into my eyes.

"Sarah?" said Lia.

"How did two such unpromising parents as we are manage to spawn such an insightful daughter?" said Sarah.

"I really don't know," said Lia. "It's so unlikely in so many ways. But I'm really proud we did."

"Me, too," said Sarah.

"And Sarah?" said Lia. "I'm sorry; I didn't know it was so hard for you."

Sarah's grin was a little crooked. "Work hard, do your homework, cheat a little when you have to," she quoted. "It all worked remarkably well. Until just this year, at least. And I blame politics and stuff for that."

"And stuff," I said, echoing the tag line as my moms had done for me when I was growing up.

So anyway, maybe I'm not actually gay. Or straight. Just... myself. Or whatever.

And come to think of it, I'm so very female that all the children I'll ever have will also be female, either XX CAIS carriers or XY CAIS women. Just like my mom and my dad. Not that Sarah likes being called Dad.

"You know," said Lia as I was about to wander away, "you don't really need a reason for whatever level of attraction you feel. It's valid whatever the reason."

I sat down again. "That's pretty profound," I said.

"Or very obvious," said Lia, smiling. "Sometimes it's hard to tell the difference."

"The most obvious things are the easiest to forget," I said. "But it's worth remembering that other people might be feeling more."

Chapter Forty-Three

Thumbing

Miranda, 2016

One of the things about being a vagabond is looking up friends (and friends of friends) of the parentals. It's a remarkably small world, and people are connected to other people who, almost without exception, don't seem to mind if I drop in on them. I don't really understand it, but hey.

I folded up my thumb and alit, as it happens not all that far from public transportation somewhere in the Boston area. Since that's not really on the way to anywhere other than maybe Maine, I figured I'd hang out for a while and then turn around and go some other way.

The phone had a number in it, so I dialed.

"Hello?"

Hooray. It was Rachael. She picked up.

"Uh, this is Miranda? MacDonald-Hartley. I think you met my moms once or something."

"Right..."

"Tysons Corner. You came to visit Rebecca Grossman and Stephan Larkin; they were our neighbors."

"I remember now, of course. You were, like..."

"Seven," I said. "So I'm a little light on the details."

"Fair enough. And I know Lia, of course. She's your mom, right? What can I do for you?"

"Oh right, she stayed with you for a while. I'm kinda thumbing around and I'm in Boston..."

"Cool," said Rachael. "You should totally come over for dinner, and, um, I'm sure we can put you up for a few days. I'll just... Right. Tell the housekeeper."

"You have a housekeeper?"

"Sort of. It's complicated. And that's such a misused way to explain anything. You've found the subway?"

"T, it says, in a big circle," I read.

"Find your way to Oak Grove. It's on the Orange Line. All the way to the end. Then call Emily. I'll text her digits to this number, shall I?"

"Text her digits... You sound like my othermother."

Rachael laughed and disconnected. These folks are old enough to be my parents. But if things here are anything like back home, they know people who know people who, should a girl get ranklings, might be able to summon up a rhapsody. Or something. All the holes in my vocabulary, but words like that just come howling through on the wind. Or something.

Pretty much everywhere I go people are just people. The accents change, the weather's a little different, but poor people in each city help out strangers, sharing what little they have. It's kind of inspiring.

Okay, so it's getting on autumn. The leaves in New England are pretty gorgeous, there's no denying that. Much better than Virginia, and they don't turn at all in Florida. I got on the subway as directed, sat down staring straight ahead, figuring it might be rude to look around. But Boston's not New York, and so I'm staring at... Well, a wardrobe malfunction waiting to happen as soon as its owner tries to adjust her backpack. Along with half the men in the car. The subway is noisy, but there are a few words when it stops and she just stares knives at the commentariat, looks at me, shrugs, and carefully doesn't move relative to the pack. Success!

"Thanks," she said, when we both got off at the last stop. Which, contrary to the name *Subway* was actually above ground.

"Sure? I think?" I said. "Can I help, like, hold your pack or whatever?"

That seemed to work, so she went one way and I went the other. Thumbed Emily's number, and waited. As promised, in 5 minutes she arrived with a boat-sized car, popped out and waved. I guess I'm the only homeless waif looking girl on the curb or something. And she brought me home with her.

She's pretty amazing. "You're the housekeeper?" I said.

"Rachael told you that?" said Emily. "Well, sort of, I guess. It's complicated."

"She said that, too," I said.

"Can I offer you the use of our laundry?"

"Oooh, that'd be cool, thank you."

We were in the basement sorting stuff into the washer when the next call came in. Rachael and, uh, somebody else, wanting rides from the station. "I swear I run a taxi service," she said, but she was smiling. "Do come along. Or maybe you'd rather get the washer started."

It was a little confusing, all the trips to the train station, which after all was just a mile; people could walk, most of them, and it wasn't even raining. But we got my laundry started.

"So, um, hi," I said, when they introduced everybody. "I'm Miranda. I met Rachael when I was a kid."

"Kids these days," somebody said, and suddenly I felt seven again, at potlucks with my moms.

"Sorry, that was mean," said Rachael. "It's part of our common banter here; it's not aimed at you."

There are six of them, and it was murder keeping track of who was who. They finish each others' sentences. They leave spaces in their sentences for somebody to fill in a word.

"So, um," I said.

"You said that already," said Rachael, smiling.

"Everybody says it's complicated when I ask about Emily and express surprise you have a housekeeper."

"Well, it's complicated," said Emily. "I was living on the street in Denver when... Well, long story. The short version is they kinda hired me to keep house. Be the house wife. Den mother. Something like that."

"That sounds pretty wonderful. Denver, huh? I haven't been that far west yet."

"Ravyn's sister lives there."

"Sort of, it's complicated," said Ravyn. She was at the head of the table. I think she's the one that somebody told me actually owns the house.

"Everything is complicated when there are lesbians around," I said. "At least in my experience."

"Girl has a point," said Rachael.

"Thanks, Emily, for the rides, the laundry soap, dinner, everything. Can I help wash up?"

"We've got it," said Emily. "But you can help if you want."

After dinner they poured me more wine and we sat in the living room together. It's very odd, seeing six grown women sitting in about four chairs, leaving one for just me. I started to protest, but they insisted they like it that way.

It's kinda rad, being treated as an equal by lesbians who are my parents' age.

"So, um," I said, suppressing a yawn. Bumming around America is hard work.

"You keep saying that," said Rachael. She was kind of half on top of Emily. And she's tiny. So is Ravyn, and, um, they told me her name was JJ? I of course thought Rachael would be big because she seemed that way the last time I saw her. When I was, like, seven.

"Sleeping arrangements, right," said Ravyn. "We, uh..."

"Fuck," said Joy.

"Sleep together," said Ravyn. "Joy is the resident Tourette's person. We let her do most of the cussing."

"Handy to have around, I'd say," I said.

"There's a twin bed in the attic. I'll put it together for you," said Emily. And she brought me upstairs.

Sure enough, there are three bedrooms, three beds, none of them made up. Emily stopped off at the linen closet, picked out some bedding, and some towels, and we went up another flight of stairs.

"I slept up here, when I first came," she said. "It's nice; heat rising through the house keeps it toasty warm. You can crack open a window if it's too much."

"You moved downstairs," I said. I should at least have made it a question.

"I guess I got a first-class upgrade or something. It's pretty irresistible, if you're inclined that way. We try not to involve the next generation. Mostly we succeed."

"Mostly." Again with the prying into other people's business. People who were kind enough to give me a place to stay for a while.

"It's pretty wild, I guess. In a sedate way. A slow riot. Or something," said Emily. "I've stopped making sense. There's just the one bathroom, and it's all the way downstairs, off the kitchen. You might want to shower tonight, since five professors will be doing it tomorrow morning, trying to get off to work."

Doing it... trying to get off... Things echoed around in my head. Thankfully, I didn't repeat them aloud.

"What are you smiling about?" Emily asked.

"The very idea... a house full of my moms, only there are six of you."

"It's pretty amazing. It's even more amazing that it works pretty well," said Emily.

There were sounds in the night that my imagination insisted had to be sexual. The moms didn't really indulge very much, not the last few years anyway. I guess having teenagers around kind of dampers things. And then there's the fact that Sarah is pretty serious and Lia is nuts.

Which kinda didn't show up til my accident. "Shit got real, yo," is the way Sarah explained the changed family dynamics to somebody she works with who wanted to help. One of those therapist types who's not a physio.

These women, though... they seem sane, and they're always laughing together, often at each other. It's just, I don't know, natural, or something. For them, anyway.

It was pretty wonderful, though, having an actual bed with clean sheets and towels and everything. And Emily kind of wanted to mother me, without actually interfering with what I'm doing. I guess being homeless as opposed to just wandering makes a person worry about her fellow humans. Especially the female ones who don't seem to have any place to go.

But not having any place to go is different from not going any place in particular. I can make it up as I go along. There's some savings from Key West, though how I managed that while living in the most expensive few square miles in the country I'll never figure out. And Sarah funds me when I'm in a pinch. I think she feels bad that the family went to pieces. Or something.

Chapter Forty-Four

School

Miranda, 2016

"You really should finish school," Ravyn told me one morning over breakfast.

The place is a madhouse on weekdays, with five professors blowing through the kitchen on the way to their turns in the shower. Together, often, which kind of blew my mind. And not the same pairs every morning.

"Maybe Emily can help you research the GED test today," she said. She poured the rest of her coffee down her throat, snagged Joy on her way through and went to the shower.

"All that... togetherness," I said, looking after her.

"Well, it is more efficient," said Emily. "Unless..."

"Yeah." I said, not wanting to have the rest of that conversation with somebody who was essentially a stranger, a member of the household in question, and likely a participant some days. Weekdays, she gets breakfast and stays out of the way til it's time to take people to the train. And then she comes home, cleans house, washes dishes, and when the hot water heater has caught up again, takes a bath. Long and leisurely. By herself, I need to add, for this household.

So it turns out you can take an exam that counts like graduating from high school, which I had missed out on because of the almost dead thing. And they have study guides and sample exams and stuff, so I spent most of a week looking through all the stuff Emily and I found. Some things I could do, and for the rest, there was a whole house full of professors. Joy and Rachael taught me to read poetry and enjoy history. Ravyn pushed me through algebra. JJ amused me with physics problems, getting more and more complicated as I got the hang of it, and of the math Ravyn was teaching me. Andi was available for answering questions, but apparently she doesn't really use the same teaching techniques JJ does, so there were some confused times, trying to ask her about JJ's homework problems.

And Emily was there the whole time, smiling, cooking amazing food, and being the mom I had missed out on during the last year or so of chaos.

After what seems to be the manner of lesbians everywhere, they knew a lot of other queer people. In some cases, their students were shacked up together. So there was ample opportunity (at pot lucks, yes) to meet women who were more my own age.

And then Lia came to town. Apparently she had talked one of the universities around the Boston area into giving her a hearing, since she had been terminated not for academic cause but just for being gay. Which, in the People's Republic, is something that happens to other people, far away, and we just don't understand it. So we hire those folks to come teach here.

There was some kind of a conference at a hotel downtown, which brought Stephan and Becca to Boston for a week or so. They brought Jim along. We had been friends when we were kids. But it turned out he was a boy and we hadn't quite gotten over that when... I had my accident.

It was good to see him, fun to hang out with him, do museums, just ride the trains around, talk to the penguins at the Aquarium, stuff like that. And then Stephan and Jim went home, and Becca came to stay with us for the weekend. "Us" in the "them but not me" sense.

Emily and I talked about it afterwards, and we agreed that sleeping with your ex is not usually a good idea. But that Becca kind

of needed it. And when your ex's ex runs The Little Sisters of the Holy Fuck (seriously, they call themselves that), well, come right in, the bed's warm.

I've seen enough middle-aged lesbian flesh to last me until I'm that age myself, I think.

Susie was living with Sarah in Maryland someplace.

Lia was... couch surfing, in a genteel kind of a way. The moms sold the house next to Becca and Stephan's place, since none of us wanted to live in Tysons Corner, or anywhere else in Virginia, ever again. It was tough for her, trying to get her mind together, until she turned up in Boston and was offered a job.

So we, and by "we" here I mean all seven of us who lived in Ravyn's house, helped her find an apartment that was more or less affordable. Rachael's old place where she'd been living when she was here had lapsed. Not paying rent on that helped some with Rachael's finances, I gather. It's a nice place and all, but kind of expensive to live here. Unless you get lucky and find a place in the garret somewhere.

And I passed my exam, and they pushed me to apply to some of the colleges around. It's really cool to have such a supportive bunch of folks at home. Maybe there's something about massively plural marriage, or not being married at all, that defuses the tension that Sarah and Lia felt, trying to live like straight people in a straight world. Also not being ultimately responsible for each other or for kids, I think? Maybe? I mean they would, all of them, be right there if something happened.

And I do know a thing or two about the somethings that can happen.

"So," said Ravyn, when I got in to the university. "If you're going to hang out with us for years as opposed to just until whatever, maybe we should draw up some documents. So we can supervise medical care, for example."

"That would be great," I said. "I mean, Lia's not far away, but."

"Lia, but," Ravyn summarized, with a knowing smile.

"You may be wanting a love life of your own sometime," Emily said.

"Living here will certainly make college more affordable," said Ravyn. "But we'd understand if you wanted to live somewhere else."

"With women your own age, for example," said Joy.

"Or men," said Rachael.

"Thanks," I said. "But I'm not really all that excited about a partner of my own right now."

"So that works, then," said Ravyn. "But we need to know if it stops working. We talk about everything in this household. I'm sure you've noticed."

"Fuck you," said Joy, just because she's Joy.

"Later," said Ravyn, grinning. "See?"

I had to laugh. It's so cute, but it's also serious business.

Chapter
Forty-Five

Managing

Mo, 2016

Things were, at least potentially, a little hot in Tysons Corner after all that went down. There's something uncomfortable about blackmail, even if it's mutual.

Sarah and Lia sold the house in Virginia. Sarah had an apartment in the Maryland burbs, but with her piece of the proceeds, she bought a house and invited Cris and me to move in with her in a nice neighborhood not too far from the newly extended Metro. So that would work. We'd be far enough away that James wouldn't feel the need to keep track of us, or we, him. But I could still get to Walter Reed and see my guys, and work with the ones who were out on the street. The place itself was funky and clearly a tale that grew in the telling. Much like the denizens.

From Sarah's point of view, Lia was past tense. We managed to put together a string of places she could stay for a week or a month at a time, and, well, it's her tale to tell, but we encouraged her to apply for academic jobs again. Someplace with job discrimination protection for gay people. Even if not for the rest of us queer folk. Perhaps, in time, it will come.

The stupid part of all this is that the summer after, when Lia was moving to Boston for her new job, gay marriage was declared legal by the old men (and now three women!) downtown. In all 50 states. But of course you could still be fired for coming out, and getting legally married without coming out might be problematic. Baby steps. Equally stupid is the fact that Cris and I could have gotten legally married any time if we wanted to, because, for Virginia purposes, he's female and I'm male, and that's really all it takes. Never mind that I'm transsexual and she's transgendered in some other way.

We make a good team, watching each others' backs. I don't know that we'd make a good couple. Or even what that is, really.

A lot of my boys are married, or were married, or tried marriage and failed when their heads exploded. Traditional marriage is as dangerous as the battlefield, I think. The casualty rates might be higher.

"Half of all marriages end in divorce," Cris said once. "Which means the other half end in murder."

It was a joke, but it's a pretty hollow one.

Susie was a sweetie, and she rolled with the changes in her life. Sarah's not all that cuddly of a mom, but she is attentive, and with several other adults around, The Sooz never wanted for affection. But we watched her for signs of trauma, something I'm way too good at picking up.

Now and then we would meet her foster parents at a burger joint or something, just to catch up. They had a couple new foster kids that Susie liked. "It's hard, letting go, but it's always good when they get to go back to their own parents," said Mr Culpeper at one of those gatherings. Which we always held safely on our side of the river.

We had a spare bedroom various people used for offices, and now and then we cleaned our junk out of it and let Miranda sleep there if she was visiting. And then one day there was a knock at the door and I answered to find a young woman, looking confused, with tears on her face.

"Hi," I said. "Come in off the street."

"Thank you," she said.

We dried her eyes and served her tea. "I'm Constance Johnson," she said. "Miranda called me George, just because it amused her, genderbending people like that."

"Our Miranda?"

"I think so... MacDonald-Hartley, she told me her last name was. I was vacationing in Key West, ran into her near the beach, decided not to go home, and..."

"And Zapwhampow, true love," I suggested.

"Well, love anyway," said George. "It was good enough for long enough, I guess."

"When Miranda texted me about somebody named George, I went, well, huh. We got into this mess because Miranda is a lesbian. Or at least she thought so at the time."

George chuckled. "She's a lesbian, all right."

"The name seems to fit you," I said.

"You must be Susie," said George, when the youngest member of the household walked in and sat down. "You remind me so much of Miranda."

"Everybody says that," said Susie. "I miss her."

"I do too," said George.

"You guys could go visit your other mom," I suggested. "Yours, Susie, not George. Miranda and Lia live, what, five miles away from each other."

"Ooh. That'd be fun," said Susie. "Can I really?" she asked

Sarah, who was sitting morosely in the corner.

"Mmm?" said Sarah. "Sorry, I wasn't paying attention."

"Can I go to Boston with George to visit Miranda and Mama?" Susie repeated. "Pleeeease?"

"Are you going, too?" Sarah said, looking at me.

"If you want me to, sure," I said. "I'm the family bodyguard."

"Family Atomics, like in Dune," said Cris.

"Pretty much. We try not to reveal too much of our hand," I said.

"Yes," said Cris. I love this person of few words and infinite potential.

"Family is such a strange concept for queer people," said George.

"Truer words were never spoken," said Sarah. "And sure, if you want to go visit, you may." She covered her ears, grinning, against the shrieks of ecstasy emitted by someone who was almost old enough to control herself. It's important to let the kid be a kid while she's a kid. There'll be plenty of time for being a grown-up later.

After we packed George and Susie off to bed, I poured Scotch for Sarah and Cris.

"Are you okay?" I asked, quietly, and sat down to listen.

"No," said Sarah.

"If you had said yes, I would have asked, as Lia taught me, 'Should I believe you?' And you would probably have been annoyed at the reminder."

Sarah smiled a little bit, reluctantly.

Made in the USA
Monee, IL
15 July 2020

36609901R00134